LONG NIGHT
DANCE

LONG NIGHT DANCE

Betsy James

E. P. DUTTON

New York

Chapter-opening decorations by Betsy James

Library of Congress Cataloging-in-Publication Data

James, Betsy.
    Long night dance/by Betsy James. — 1st ed.
        p.   cm.
    Summary: Sixteen-year-old Kat, child of a scandalous, disastrous
marriage between a Hill woman and an Upslope man, rescues a
Rigi man from the sea during the week of the Long Night Dance
and begins to realize a person's value does not come from his
background or appearance.
    ISBN 0-525-44485-8
    [1. Fantasy.   2. Prejudices—Fiction.]   I. Title
PZ7.J15357Lo 1989   88-38837
[Fic]—dc19   CIP
                                                                  AC

Published in the United States by E. P. Dutton,
a division of Penguin Books USA Inc.

Published simultaneously in Canada by
Fitzhenry & Whiteside Limited, Toronto

Designer: Barbara Powderly

Printed in the U.S.A.   First Edition   10 9 8 7 6 5 4 3 2 1

LONG NIGHT DANCE

Betsy James

E. P. DUTTON

New York

Chapter-opening decorations by Betsy James

Library of Congress Cataloging-in-Publication Data
James, Betsy.
  Long night dance/by Betsy James.—1st ed.
    p. cm.
  Summary: Sixteen-year-old Kat, child of a scandalous, disastrous
marriage between a Hill woman and an Upslope man, rescues a
Rigi man from the sea during the week of the Long Night Dance
and begins to realize a person's value does not come from his
background or appearance.
  ISBN 0-525-44485-8
  [1. Fantasy. 2. Prejudices—Fiction.] I. Title
PZ7.J15357Lo 1989   88-38837
[Fic]—dc19   CIP
                                                            AC

Published in the United States by E. P. Dutton,
a division of Penguin Books USA Inc.

Published simultaneously in Canada by
Fitzhenry & Whiteside Limited, Toronto

Designer: Barbara Powderly

Printed in the U.S.A.   First Edition   10 9 8 7 6 5 4 3 2 1 *for Chris*

THE RIGI'S SONG

I am a man upon the land,
I am a beast upon the deep,
I am the fin that hides the hand,
I am the dream that riddles sleep.

I am the wind that breaks the door,
I am the pulse that fans the pain,
I am the wave that grinds the shore,
I am the rock that turns the rain.

I am the flesh that loves the flame,
I am the fur that loves the wave,
I am the cloak, I am the name,
I am the bright blood and the grave.

I am the skin that sleeks the bone,
I am the sun on the black sea.
I am the heart that heals the stone.
Come to me! Come to me!

I

IT WAS A CRAZY PLACE to have built a house, on
the western cliffs where the wind was incessant, but
Ab Drem had gotten the land cheaply in trade.
Upslope approved of wind: It blew the nonsense out
of you. Ab Drem had been seeking to recover the
approval of Upslope for more than twenty years,
ever since the scandal about his wife, and it was a
point in his favor that he lived in an abominably
windy house. And that he kept it so clean—although
of course it was his daughter, Katyesha, who kept it
clean.

It was Kat who saw to all of Cliff Tooth House,

3

since like most Upslope men Ab Drem was often
away from home, dealing up and down the coastal
trade routes in brandy and tobacco, molasses and
cinnamon and gold. Kat swept his hearth and made
his porridge, mended the elbows of his good jacket
and polished his boots. She milked the cow for her
older brother, Dai. She coaxed a stunted garden
from the windswept earth of the cliff top. She
fetched rainwater from the cistern with the yoke,
and baked brown bread; she went to market. She
scrubbed. But all that was what one would expect
from a daughter or a wife. She was only a woman,
after all.

Kat was small and brown-armed, with a grim
golden face freckled like a speckled egg. Her hair
was curly and furiously, ragingly red; but it was cut
short. Auntie Jerash cut it and made her hide it
under a clean gray linen kerchief, because it was like
her mother's hair.

This afternoon Kat tied the kerchief reluctantly;
she was to meet Auntie Jerash at the crossroads and
go Downshore to market. Now that she was sixteen
she did the household marketing by herself, but this
was the week of the Long Night dance that marked
the beginning of winter, and the native harbor town
seethed with carnival. It would not be decent for an
Upslope woman to be seen there alone. Upslope did
not celebrate Long Night.

Catching up her basket, Kat latched the door
behind her, tying her cloak as she ran. The wind
from the cliff that was called Horn Loft blew her

along toward the crossroads like a leaf; she glanced back uneasily into the teeth of it.

She did not want to go to market with Auntie Jerash. But if she stayed home she would have to wrestle with herself about going down to the seals' beach at the foot of the cliff. For two days she had thought of nothing else.

It called her; but she would not listen anymore. Respectable people from Upslope did not go to the beach. They never went near the sea. Why, from that black water who knew what might rise? There were stories. . . .

Because of her mother, Kat had to be very careful to be respectable. Putting the wind at her back, she ran toward the crossroads. But she could not run faster than her thoughts; in her mind she saw the gray measureless horizon, the long gray waves.

"Cover your head!" hissed Auntie Jerash.

Kat snatched at her kerchief with a gasp; the wind had blown it half away. Dreaming, she had come to the main road, and Auntie Jerash stood waiting in her stiff gray linen, very cross.

"Yes, ma'am." As Kat tucked her red curls out of sight she bundled that memory of beach, with its windy singing, back down into the darkest cupboard of her heart.

"You are late," said Auntie Jerash. "A good house-keeper is never late." She turned in her voluminous hooded cloak and surged out among the traffic.

With looks of pitying scorn, her six pale daughters trotted after her. They were obedient in public,

5

vindictive in private: They hissed and pinched, like geese. When Kat's mother died, her aunt had taken her in out of duty, for someone must teach her to be a wife. Among her cousins Kat had learned to pinch, to kick ankles under the table, and to smile graciously. There was no need for her to learn to cipher or to read. When she could manage a kitchen by herself, she had been sent back to her father, who had dismissed his housekeeper with real relief, for it had been an expense.

Kat hurried to catch up with the line of immaculate, drab hoods, whispering savagely to the smallest and last in line, "Missa! A good housekeeper doesn't scuffle with her shoes."

There were many strangers on Scythe Road, all natives—on foot, on muleback or in carts, traveling down to the carnival. From the safety of her hood Kat stared at Downshore men in high red stockings, River men with their trousers rolled, Lake people with reed bundles on their backs. There were women with red hair; Kat did not look at them but made sure of her kerchief and watched her feet. The road slanted down the cliffs in steep switchbacks. Raising her head suddenly, she saw the sea: From this height it looked safe, flat and clean, the sun polishing it like a flagstone floor.

The groaning wheel of a brewer's cart arced past their small procession, leaving a frond of mud across the hem of Missa's skirt.

Missa began to snivel and whine.

"There!" said Auntie Jerash. "Katyesha, keep your cousin from the dirt. A good housekeeper . . ."

A wagonload of squealing hogs lurched past her into a puddle.

"Filthy harbor town!" cried Auntie Jerash.

In a straggling line they entered Downshore, Kat pushing Missa ahead of herself into the widening alleyway paved haphazardly with cobbles and earth. The air smelled of ocean, of manure, of geraniums and sausage and mud. Missa still whined. "Be still," said Kat. "It's only dirt."

The whine became a snarl, and Missa reached back to get in a good pinch. When Kat dodged her, Missa whispered with venom, "Your mother had red hair. Your mother was a Hill woman!"

"Katyesha!" said Auntie Jerash. "At your age. Leave that child alone."

Before them Downshore unrolled its festival canopies, striped sails much torn but still brilliant in yellow and orange and green. Vendors were raising the braziers that would scarcely cool all week, setting the older children to grate cabbage and onions while the younger ones shrieked and tangled among the table legs. The children were barefoot in the cool sunlight, bright in their colored shirts. They sang. In Upslope no one sang; it was wicked.

Carpenters squabbled and hallooed; a pig squealed for the butcher; a cat slept calmly on a heap of turnips. As Kat watched, a blue clay mug of beer jittered itself off the end of a hammered plank and burst on the cobblestones; a lame dog trotted over to lap at the puddle.

"Don't touch anything," ordered Auntie Jerash. "Pray that someday Upslope will have a proper market and decent women won't need to come down here at all."

They went straight to the fish stalls. A girl behind the wet boards, her fat baby on her hip, handed Kat the week's fish—a perch, always the same. The girl smiled and said "Thank you!" for the brass coin, but Kat did not answer, stowing the fish in her basket.

They were turning toward the vegetable stalls when a young native hunter, unloading skins for trade, swung a bundle from his shoulder and caught Auntie Jerash squarely on the back.

"Sorry, ma'am!" He pushed back his cloth cap and grinned.

But Kat had seen: They were sealskins.

"Dirty native!" cried Auntie Jerash. "Children, come! We shall do without vegetables." Herding them sternly back toward Scythe Road she announced rigidly through her teeth, "I shall never, I say *never* again come Downshore to this pigsty on the week of the Long Night dance!"

Out of earshot, Missa turned on Kat her prim, vindictive face. "Your mother was a native!" she whispered. "Your mother bore a demon child!"

Kat took her by the back of her cloak and hoisted her until she stood on tiptoe. "Stop it," she hissed, "or the Rigi will call you away and drag you down where the sea is blackest, and drown you dead!"

"*Mama!*"

"Katyesha!" cried Auntie Jerash. And then, with a shrug: "But what would one expect?"

2

IT WAS TRUE that Kat's mother was a Hill woman. She was still much discussed in Upslope, in lowered voices. Ab Drem had brought her back with him from his first trip to the hills, in the days when he was a wild lad and still only Drem; he had brought her openly, defiantly, already big with his child. She had been beautiful, as Auntie Jerash explained the wicked often are, but that first child was a demon, born with a bear's face, and lived only a day.

In the horror of remorse Drem had made it right: Though she was a native, he had made her his wife and had taken the name Ab that meant he was a married man. He had been a good husband. He had never beaten her, though she deserved it, nor the two children who came later. She had fallen silent and covered her bright hair.

"And then she died," said Kat aloud. That was how Auntie Jerash always ended the story. "She died."

Kat was straggling back drearily toward Horn Loft in the early dusk. The beach would be dark; she barricaded her mind against it. Ahead of her, Cliff Tooth House showed no light and she could feel, even before she got there, its silence. Ab Drem would not be home until tomorrow, and Dai was at the native tavern at Rake, talking earnestly about cows. Poor Dai! He did not have a bear's face, but he had a beard, which in Ab Drem's eyes was an evil nearly equal. Dai loved cows, he was no merchant and no mathematician, he bumbled in to dinner with manure on his boots, and he could not play War. Dai was part of the punishment for their mother, like Kat's red hair.

To withstand the wind at Cliff Tooth House, the door latch was stiff; because her hands were full and Ab Drem was not there to berate her for it, Kat stood on one foot and kicked it open. The wind came in with her, snouting through Ab Drem's neat account books. At the edge of the door frame it sang a phantom music.

Kat slammed the door and set her back to it. "It's her fault!" She spoke aloud in the dark house. "She was a native! Good women don't walk on the beach.

They don't sing." By the dull red glow of the coals the ancient tomcat roused himself stiffly, then sat down again as though it were too much trouble, and closed his eyes. The wind ceased, becoming dull house air.

Aside from the scatter of ash on the white hearth tiles, the one-room house was, as always, immaculate. Even in that meager firelight everything shone, white or black; the hearth itself, improbably white and bare, was scrubbed daily by herself, often twice. The curtains hung without a wrinkle. The straight-backed black chairs were set precisely at the table; the plain doors of the black, cupboardlike box beds—one each for Ab Drem, Kat, and Dai—gleamed dully. Even the wood box glinted. Though there was only one room, it was big enough to be shadowy, shining, cold.

Taking up the poker, Kat beat the fire into a blaze. She found the polishing rag and tightened the gray kerchief over her curls. Standing on the bare, dusty hearth she said, "What must I do?"

Hitch the yoke to the oaken water pails and fill them at the cistern.

Fetch the fish from the market basket.

Sweep the hearth, mop the floor.

Set straight the stool, the stiff black chairs and the stiff black table that were always already straight.

Dust everything that needed dusting; because of the ashes and the wind and the whiteness of the room, everything always needed dusting.

Polish Ab Drem's best boots, the wood box, the black box beds; her mother's dowry chest; each single porcelain piece of Ab Drem's priceless game of War, even though he kept them tucked up in the worn, velvet-lined drawer and they needed no dusting. Well, polish everything.

Was that all? Kat at the mantel put her forehead down suddenly onto her bare brown arms, thinking: There has to be something else, because I feel all the time that this is not enough.

Again the memory rose around her like a wave: gray shore, gray sea.

"There's plenty of firewood," Kat said in despair. "I won't go!"

She had always told herself that it was for the sake of the driftwood that she went to the beach. Firewood cost money, and to gather it herself was thrifty. Ab Drem, of course, never knew she went there; he thought it was Dai who brought the wood.

But Kat went to the beach because of the Rigi's song.

She had been twelve and she had gone Downshore to market with Auntie Jerash. She was in one of her bleeding times that were only a few months started; she could not refuse the journey because she would have had to say why, so she followed in the wake of the older cousins with her hood pulled over her face.

But no sooner had they come to the market square than the pain grew so great that she had to stand in a sunny corner and put her hand on the stone wall to steady herself; her aunt guessed her out in a moment and said with irritation, "Dirty child! Next time you'll have the sense to keep it at home. Sit, and we'll come back for you. Now don't touch anything." And she gathered her whispering brood and hustled off toward the fish stalls.

Kat sat on the wooden public bench next to a very plump old lady with a basket of apples. Like Auntie Jerash, the women looked at Kat shrewdly and said, "Your time, dearie? Sometimes it does take sharp."

Kat ducked her head, drowned in shame. She kept her ankles together and her elbows in, trying not to touch the bench. The pain came in waves, and she wondered what would happen if she threw up.

Around her the rowdy market crowd jostled and cried—vendors and fishwives and calling children. But after a while the bench, backed up by the warm old stone, began to feel safe; the pain in her womb and back unclenched and smoothed, and she straightened herself with a long breath.

Because the pain had stopped, the world looked holy, and tranquil, and dear. From one of the gray stone alleys behind her came the sound of a drum.

It was someone tuning a drum, actually—trying one beat, stopping to tighten the goat hide and trying one beat again. She could see neither drum nor drummer. Then it seemed to be set right, for after a few taps and rattles the drum took up a steady tempo, the beat of the resting heart. It boomed alone until it knew its rhythm absolutely, as the heart slows and steadies after running, and then over it rose a solitary voice, singing:

I am a man upon the land,
I am a beast upon the deep,
I am the fin that hides the hand,
I am the dream that riddles sleep.

I am the wind that breaks the door,
I am the pulse that fans the pain,
I am the wave that grinds the shore,
I am the rock that turns the rain.

I am the flesh that loves the flame,
I am the fur that loves the wave,
I am the cloak, I am the name,
I am the bright blood and the grave.

I am the skin that sleeks the bone,
I am the sun on the black sea.
I am the heart that heals the stone.
Come to me! Come to me!

The voice was clear, absolute, male. Over the dark boom of the drum it flashed like a knife. Taken unaware, Kat felt it, saw it: the land, the deep, the bright male face, the beast.

"What is that?" Forgetting her aunt's warnings, she took hold of the apple woman's arm with both hands. "Please, what is he singing?"

"Eh?" The woman was gossiping with a friend at

14

her other elbow. "That song? Why . . . ah, but you're Upslope, poor thing. That's the Rigi's song, for Long Night."

"The Rigi! The . . . the Rigi drown you." Kat was taken aback. Auntie Jerash used the Rigi as a threat: a vague animal blackness, teeth and claws. "They bring bad dreams."

"Pish!" sniffed the old woman. The singing had continued, and Kat listened; the drum shuddered in the stones, and it was as though her body listened, not her ears.

"The Rigi," said the apple woman firmly, "live at the world's edge, west over the water where the boats won't go. They are seals. They wear sealskins, they dance the Seal. They brought the first song of all to us, and now you hear it. It's the song for crossing, the Rigi's song for Long Night."

"They're *seals*?"

"They're men and women, dearie, like all of us. But when they dance, they're seals."

The song and the drumming had stopped. Kat realized that she was clutching the old woman's arm and took her hands away, not so hastily as she might have. She told herself fiercely, "I have to remember that. I have to remember."

"Here you are, love." The apple woman gave her a little pippin, very hard and very red. "You do look better. Next moon remember: tea of raspberry leaf, if there's anything so kindly to be had up there." She rose to go. "Or come to me and I'll give you some. I keep the herb stall down beyond the portals, and nobody but Mailin knows more healing than

15

me." She laughed and patted Kat's face. "I'm an otter when I dance," she said, and trotted off across the square.

Kat knew she ought to drop the apple down behind the bench and leave it. But she hid it in the bodice of her blouse, and pulled up her brown cloak. Her aunt came back with the girls, still scolding, and together they walked back up Scythe Road. Kat put the apple under the mattress of her box bed, and that night, while Dai and Ab Drem snored distantly in dreams, she sat up in the close dark and ate it, seeds and all, right down to the stem. It tasted tart and very clean. In the morning she threw the stem into the fire.

Kat had never said anything about the Rigi. The song—now worn and altered by years of carrying—was one of the few things that were her own. Piecing together what little she could remember, she had sung it over and over, never aloud, turning it like a box that has the whole world in it but no key.

Indeed it had seemed to her that it grew, filling all the spaces of the days—that as she scrubbed the shirts it sang itself to her; as she kneaded the brown bread the song kept the rhythm; as she made the butter the music rose and fell as though her hand held a drumstick instead of the dasher of the churn.

It sang itself most loudly when she went down to the beach, because the seals were there; and little by little Kat had begun to be afraid. As Auntie

Jerash explained the relative order of men and animals, with somewhere between them natives and wives, Kat had seen that the Rigi's song, like all singing, was bad. It was her mother's blood badness that called her to it. And she must be good, obedient and meek, or whose name would she wear when Ab Drem was dead?

So she had stopped singing it; but it would not be stopped. The song called her to the beach. When she got there it was waiting for her. She had to exhaust herself by carrying the biggest drifted logs, under the pretense that they were for Ab Drem's meeting-day fire, before the song would be quiet. And for the last two days, as the Long Night approached, the call of the beach had been nearly a command; the song rose all about her, as seals rise suddenly to crowd an empty sea.

Standing in the shadowy house, Kat cried, "I *won't* go to the beach. I'm a grown woman. Someday I'll be married, and that will be respectable."

She turned back to the housework that was always the same, stopping to stroke the old cat's tail. It was bony and rough like a string of spools. His name was Small Gray; when he was a kitten he would bat her hands with his paws, but not anymore. He slept.

So the evening went, solitary as always, for the evening was solitary even when Ab Drem and Dai were there. Dai rarely spoke. If he had had a pint or two, he might play Scissors Paper Stone, or make paws of his hands and pretend to box her as Small Gray used to, but more and more he didn't even come home to his box bed but curled up in the straw of the byre with the cow, where it was friendlier. He had an old blanket there.

"So what," Kat said aloud. "Stupid cow."

She dropped the polishing cloth on the hearth and kicked it into the fire. Banking the coals, she undressed in the dark, struggling blind into her white nightgown. She did not stroke Small Gray to say good night but unlatched the doors of her box bed, crawled in, and latched them after herself, saying nothing, feeling nothing.

She lay stiff on the cold mattress. After a long time it began to feel more kindly. There was no one to hear her, and she lay face down on the pillow in the dark, crying, kicking the old box bed. "I don't like it! I don't want it!"

But what it was that she didn't like and didn't want, she didn't know. "Stop it! Stop it!" she sobbed into the pillow, and stopped kicking, and fell asleep.

3

SHE WOKE IN THE DARKNESS, hearing drums.

It was not drums, of course, but the wind, booming down the chimney. Sometimes it could sound like a drum, sometimes like snakes, and sometimes like human voices crying.

Kat sat up in the motionless dark and gathered the comforter around her shoulders. Her body knew that it was early, early morning, still lightless but beginning to be day. The air in the box bed was close and still, while in the chimney of the empty house the wind boomed and sobbed. It was a drum, a drum! Huge and gloomy, the dark was trying to get into the clean white box of the house, into the box bed.

From the edge of dream, in that unguarded instant before waking, it seemed natural to Kat that there should be a drum in the dark. Wasn't it almost the Long Night? She was not afraid. She listened for the song but she could not hear it. Her defenses were down; she was exhausted with shoring them up. She thought: Somebody should sing the Rigi's song for that drum.

"All right," she said aloud, as one might placate an animal or a child. "I'll sing."

She began, as always, to sing silently in her mind.

In the stuffy dark of the box bed, the song seemed sad and dead. That made her angry. So in her sweet, tuneless voice she sang the song aloud for the first time.

I am a man upon the land,
I am a beast upon the deep, . . .

The song was too big for the box bed. Without thinking, she lifted the latch and pushed open the doors into the drafty room, swinging her bare legs over the edge of the mattress.

The song dressed her, hustled her through the barren house with its stiff furniture and banked fire, opened the door, and carried her into the night that was turning toward morning. It carried her past the sleeping byre to the narrow path which goats' feet and her own had made to Horn Loft. When it had her faced well into the wind and blown more full of

20

breath than she had ever been in her life, it tore the kerchief from her head and said, "Sing!"

She clung to a rough spur of rock and sang as loudly as she could.

> *I am a man upon the land,*
> *I am a beast upon the deep,*
> *I am the fin that hides the hand,*
> *I am the dream that riddles sleep.*

The wind blew all of it right away from her. It was a wild, spendthrift feeling, like throwing money into the air and watching it blow backwards over all creation. Her chest felt spacious, light; she opened her arms into the wind and shouted, just to shout.

"I am!" she yelled. "Kat!" The wind stole her name as well. Something was still wanting; giddy with liberty, she shouted outrageously, "I'm going to the beach!"

The waning moon blinked among the scudding clouds, and Kat could see perfectly, as though the sea itself gave off some light. She trotted along the cliff to the stony cleft where the path down Horn Loft began. There the pine woods came right down to the cliffs and it was woodsy and hushed, the wind baffled by the stunted trees. A trickling seep ran out of it, down the rocks. Trying not to think of bears, Kat turned right, away from the woods; the path broke out of the scrubby pines and opened onto the cliff face, heading down.

She had walked this path a thousand times, though never before in the dark. She did not dare look out over the bleak sea far below, but watched her boots. The wind did not buffet her. It blew steadily, so that when she stumbled she was held against the stone as though by a hand.

When she reached the water the wind eased. At the cliffs' foot the sea had built itself a steep, curved strand of pebbles and coarse gray sand; the black tide seethed among the scattered rocks and skerries. This beach was no harbor. No one but the seals was ever here—in any weather—and whenever Kat came they fled to the boulders in the surf or bobbed their sleek heads in the leaden sea. Over the years she had watched them sharply to see whether one might take off its skin, but that had never happened. Now in the gleam that seemed to come from the sea itself, even the rocks were empty. The beach was as sweetly round as the fish scale moon, and wholly hers.

It was deliciously wicked to be out in the middle of the night. To be by the sea added a zest of danger: Might fangs rise from it, a lazy tentacle coil? Kat found a strong straight stick for hitting things with. For all her wandering on the beach, she had never touched the water. She had heard that it was salty, like blood. Now she kept to the tide mark as usual, where the driftwood lay in piles.

This was an even better place for the song. The bursting out was over and it felt at home, neither too large nor too small, here where land and deep together had built this beach. She sauntered and sang.

I am the skin that sleeks the bone,
I am the sun on the black sea.
I am the heart that heals the stone.
Come to me! Come to me!

She found an old boot half buried in the sand and turned it over with her stick. In her gathering she had scratched up lost nets with their cork floats; broken lobster pots; an iron spoon; bits of crating branded with letters she could not read. She had found dead seals as well. Even dead they were awesome: huge-shouldered and narrow-hipped and bigger than a man, with the points of white teeth at their curved lips.

Kat halted in her strolling with a jolt; there was a dead seal on the far side of the beach right now. She cupped her hands around her eyes to squint at it, a dark hump among the wrack left by the retreating tide. Maybe it was not dead, because there was a draggled trail of fresh wet coming up from the water to where it lay.

Kat did not know whether seals were fierce, or if they bit. She stalked around the back of the tumbled logs—where a sure-footed girl in boots could hop from trunk to trunk but an angry seal could not—and peered through the dark from a prudent distance. It lay snarled in a heap of weed, big-shouldered, motionless.

Well above it on the beach a huge pine stump had been rolled in by the waves to lie with its great root-wheel in the air. Kat climbed that, to be safe.

She was not so much afraid as cautious. The seals had always fled, so this one was dead after all; but she dared not go close enough to poke it with her stick.

In an instant's cockiness she leaned out from her perch and sang, good and loud:

> *I am a man upon the land,*
> *I am a beast upon the deep, . . .*

She stopped abruptly, as the seal pushed itself up on its front flippers. It was not a seal at all, but a man.

4

IT WAS A MAN. He pushed himself up on his
elbows and turned his head slowly to either side, as
though looking for the singer; then he sank down
again with his face on the wet sand.

Kat clung to the tree trunk. A man, a man—on
her own deserted beach, a man. She had no knife,
even if she had known how to use one. Nothing
but the stick. Panic swamped her. When she could
think at all it was: He hasn't seen me yet. Be still,
still as a stone, and when he turns his head away,
run.

She pulled in her head and sat motionless, like a mouse on a barley stalk when it sees the owl.

The moon slipped in and out of the clouds, and the only sound was the roar and sigh of water. His wet back heaved with breathing. Kat saw him gather himself onto his elbows and crawl, dragging his right leg, a few yards higher on the beach before he sank down again onto his face.

"His foot's hurt," she thought immediately, and at once the advantage shifted to her side.

She made a short, impulsive gesture as though to jump straight down, but her body was wiser than her head, and slower. Using both hands and feet like the mouse, she climbed backward off the root tangle. She had no idea what to do. It was that instant of the morning when the dark first eases, and she could not be sure whether the shift in her eyes was day coming, or whether she was only wishing it to come.

She stepped around the tree stump with the stick in her hand.

He lay where he had fallen, not so big after all except for his shoulders—not much bigger than she was. He was tangled in weed, for he had crawled through the tide line like a turtle looking for warm sand. His hair was sleek with wet. She thought: He'll die of cold.

She hunkered down a yard or two away from him, holding out one end of the stick as though to fend off a snake. She said the first thing she could think of.

"Mister!"

He was up into a half squat so quickly that she dropped the stick and scuttled backward behind the tree trunk. She saw him see her; her heart slammed under her breastbone.

He dropped back heavily to kneeling. Like a pair of dogs they glared at each other. When he made no move, Kat rose cautiously and circled him, snatching up the near end of the stick and owning it again.

She thought coldly: If he jumps at me I'll knock his head off.

But he knelt, sandy and still with his back straight, his right hand on his thigh; his left wrist was crooked, as though broken, and he held it close to his body. In the faintly rising light he was, as Auntie Jerash would have said, as naked as shame itself; more than naked, for the sea had tumbled him through the boulders of the surf and he was skinned and scoured. He had the short, muscular torso of the Downshore stevedores. His face was unshaven, ugly with exhaustion, young.

In shame and confusion she could hardly look at him, but he sat quietly licking his lower lip, which bled. In a low voice raw with hope he said, "You sang that?"

The question was so unexpected that, without intending to, she lowered the stick a little. He had spoken the Plain tongue, with an accent even rounder than Downshore's.

Recovering, she raised the stick again, demanding, "What are you doing here?"

"I swam," he said.

She looked suspiciously from him to the seething water. Nobody in Upslope could swim. Was he a fisherman? To mask her ignorance, she told him, "You fell out of your boat."

He shook his head. Watching her, he said, "I swam from the Place of Bones."

She had never heard of that place. It must have shown on her face because he said gently, "It was new for me also."

But he had begun to shake. Leaning forward, he laid his right hand palm-down on the sand, the fingers spread. He asked earnestly, "Is this place safe?"

Remorse swamped her, for he was shuddering with cold. Untying her heavy cloak, she dropped it backward and began to drag her sweater over her head. She warned him, "If you touch me I'll hit you with the stick."

He stared, astonished.

Pulling her wrists free of the sweater—it was plain brown wool, no matter if he bled on it—she said, "Sit up." He sat back on his heels and she threw the sweater to him. "Put that on."

She was afraid to go any closer to him, because he was naked.

He looked at the sweater across his knees.

"Ch-h-h-h!" she said. That was one of Ab Drem's favorite curses, the fragment of a longer one which he did not permit himself, and she felt worldly to use it. "You'll die of cold. Put it on."

Fumbling, he tried to lift it; but he had spent all

his strength on staying upright, and could only hold it to his chest.

She felt stupid, cruel, bewildered. With repugnance she crept near him and took it back; he did not grab her as Auntie Jerash said men did, nor was she suddenly naked herself. He let her have it, trying to keep his back straight.

She held the sweater in both hands and spoke out of terror and compassion: "Mister . . ."

He raised his good hand and laid one finger on her wrist. She looked at it, as though it lay on a stranger's wrist. His hand was bigger than hers, square and cold. He said, "I did not mean to trespass in your own place."

"Don't be stupid," she told him, strung between fear and baffled rage. She turned the sweater around furiously to find the neck. "Don't you be stupid!"

She had dressed babies: You got the head through and then you figured out the rest. As she tugged the sweater over his wet hair she did not have to touch him; she did not want to touch him, as though being naked he must be dirty. His right arm was no problem, but when she tried to pull the thick sleeve over his broken hand he cried out.

"Oh, don't!" she said. Steeling herself, she reached down the sleeve to brace his arm against her own, and drew it through.

He did not feel dirty at all. He felt clean and very cold, like an apple.

She heard the apple woman's voice: *They're men and women, dearie, like all of us.*

29

The man was reeling as a calf does when the cow licks it. "Mister," said Kat, "are you a Rigi?"

He stared. He shook his head, and his harrowed face broke into a grin that flashed a broken canine tooth.

She thought he was laughing at her superstition, and groped angrily for her cloak. When she turned back to him, his face in the rising light was full of soft mischief; listing like a sinking ship, he held two fingers in the air.

"Two Rigi," he said. He tucked one finger away. "But one Rig," and pointed, smiling, to himself.

It was a grammar lesson. He was indeed one of the Rigi, but only one.

One Rig.

At that moment of the dawn the colors came, and she saw that his hair was brown like an otter's fur, and that his eyes were gray.

"Then you're a seal!" she whispered, and he answered, "Not anymore."

All she could think to do was to put her cloak around him. As she tied it at his neck he said suddenly, "Look. . . . Your hair is red!" He leaned forward, and would not sit back up.

The light was rising. The day looked soft and desolate, as though everything were too far apart. Sandpipers cried along the water. Soon the tide would drive all air-breathers back above its reach, except seals, who could turn and dive back into the sea.

She heard his voice at her knee and bent down to him.

30

He turned his face and said, "I will not die in this cold place."

"You have to get up," she said fiercely.

He tried to rise, but it was only a little movement. He shook his head.

Kat weighed him with her eyes against a driftwood log, against rainwater in two oaken pails.

"Never mind," she said. "I'll carry you."

He was hard to get a grip on, and after the first hundred yards he was a dead weight. But Kat had him nearly to the top of Horn Loft in the rising sun before she remembered that she might have gone for Dai.

5

AB DREM RARELY PLAYED WAR in the morning, or drank whiskey either, but at the house of his younger brother, Ab Jerash, the board was always set. He had risen very early, at that hour which is neither night nor morning, and left the inn. He had ridden into Upslope on the bony-backed mule to find Jerash and his elder brother, Ab Seroy, enjoying the end of an enormous breakfast of rashers and eggs.

Graystone House was also windy and cold—all the houses in Upslope were—but while the chimney at Cliff Tooth House howled, the one at Graystone only whined, and it was quite comfortable to rest at the drafty ingle, smoking a pipe.

Ab Drem was glad to sit down. He had been three days on the mule, which he disliked and which disliked him. His lean haunches ached and his nose was wind-bitten on his stern, unhappy face, but he would not acknowledge discomfort except by being generally irritable. Also he had not slept well. He had dreamed.

"Welcome, brother." Ab Jerash poured shots all round and set up the game with his porcelain counters, white and black. They were old and lovely, but Ab Drem thought them not so lovely as his own. His were an ancient set. Their forefathers had used them long before Upslope had come from the south to make its settlement on the cliffs, and they were plainer; the characters were effaced to general shapes, so that it was easier to see the game as numbers rather than as humans killing and being killed. Using Ab Drem's set one thought, "Two influences twelve and eliminates seven," rather than "Chancellor strikes baron and kills slave." Ab Drem allowed himself to be cautiously happy, now and then, about his own set of War.

Ab Jerash liked his board, however, and sat smiling at it. The three brothers were identically lean and stern in their tweed jackets, their gray trousers tucked into immaculate black boots. They wore gold as well, but seldom visibly—just a glint at throat or cuff. And though Ab Drem, a widower, was mended and polished by Katyesha instead of by his wife, to his credit it was said that he looked as well kept as any.

They tossed a coin between them to see who would be white, who black, and who—since there were three of them—would be spy. To his dismay Ab Drem cast spy.

"Don't take me seriously, boys," he said, running his hand over his once-fair hair. "I left my wits at the inn at Pelcommon." He loaded his pipe and dragged the tall stool over to the board, where he could survey both players.

"With a lady?" said Ab Seroy, knocking on the table for luck and beginning the game.

"No," said Ab Drem without emotion. Seroy's humor was repetitive. "Too much of that damned mule's back, too much tavern-keepers' food, not enough sleep. The usual."

"If you're not going to sleep," said Ab Seroy, "it might as well be with a lady."

"Kill," said Ab Jerash, and he took away the body of a slave.

Ab Drem flinched. He preferred the modern call, "Reduce." He said, "When I sleep I dream."

Ab Jerash watched intently as Seroy maneuvered behind his baron. "You'll remember that it was me dreaming last year. I felt as weak as a woman."

"Kill! Kill!" said Ab Seroy.

"You might have seen that coming, Drem, and told me. What kind of spy are you?"

"I tell you I'm weary," said Ab Drem. Seroy smiled, removing the bodies.

34

"I dreamed of fire." Ab Jerash glared at the board and moved his prince. "Last year—fire, fire, so much . . ."

"Kill," said Ab Seroy.

"Ch-h-h-h! Ah . . . kill." Seroy had left himself open. "It was fire. I saw the doctor for it. Took a sedative, and it passed. Now it's the gout wakes me, nothing more."

"I must see the doctor," said Ab Drem. "Look there, Jerash."

"He lies," said Ab Seroy.

"Why is he a spy, if not to lie?" said Ab Jerash. "Kill, brother. Is it fire you dream of?"

"No," said Ab Drem. He spoke reluctantly. "I dream . . . nothing."

Seroy laughed. "Then nothing keeps you awake."

"Nothing real," said Ab Drem.

"Huh!" said Ab Seroy. "If it's real then you just kill it." He winked broadly at Jerash. "The Rigi have got him!"

"Grow up, Seroy," said Ab Drem. The talk made him miserable and he regretted having begun it. Even speaking of it brought the dreams to mind: the huge sea profound and dim; the men in skins who rose from it, big-shouldered, their eyes gray as water. They gazed at him, implored; they sang. Though it seemed he knew their words, he could not make reason of them and woke sweating, thinking, Beasts! Beasts!

"The Rigi will drown you for sure," Seroy said, grinning, "unless you grab their sealskins. Their women are lovely, long hair and breasts like this,

and if you grab their skins they have to follow you."
He laughed. "You could use a woman, Drem, there's
your problem."

"Are you studying nursery tales, Seroy?" Ab Jerash
said mildly, adding, "I wouldn't follow you even if
you had my skin."

"There's those that would," said Ab Seroy amiably,
flashing the gold chain at his wrist. "Kill, kill."

"It's the doctor you want, Drem," said Ab Jerash,
"and get that girl of yours to make camomile tea
before bedtime. Camomile and rum."

"No rum," said Ab Drem. "It gives me a headache."

"So do the Rigi," said Ab Seroy. "You're no spy
at all. Jerash has killed me. When will you find a
husband to manage that girl?"

"When I find a good one," said Ab Drem shortly.
"And she doesn't need managing. I've seen to that."

"Ch-h-h! All women need managing. Kill." Seroy
cleared away the body and banged the dottle from
his pipe onto the floor for the wife to sweep up. "I'll
tell you something of use. Ab Harlan's broken the
betrothal of his youngest son."

"Has he!" said Ab Drem with genuine interest.

"Fell out with the girl's father, Ab Stainis in
Pelcommon, over the wine contract."

"The youngest. Which boy is that?"

"Damned if I remember," said Ab Seroy. "He has
as many cockerels as you have hens, Jerash. Have
the two of you nothing better to do at night? All
of them look alike. Big lads, heavy, like their father."

"He'll be worth a lot in connections even if he

has not a penny to him," said Ab Jerash, "which is not the case. Ab Harlan! How old is your girl now, Drem?"

"Fourteen. No, fifteen. Well, sixteen it might be."

"Can't you handle your accounts? Anyway, she's of an age to marry, and I believe the boy's the same—fifteen. Bind the girls up young and get them settled with a child, it's safer; there's always time for boys' wildness. You talk to Harlan, brother, see that you do."

"I doubt he'd have me," said Ab Drem with deliberate pain. "Not Harlan. I have goods enough these days, but there's the matter of the child's mother."

"Be damned, her mother," said Ab Jerash. "It's you Harlan needs, and your goods, and into the bargain he gets a little chit to give him grandchildren. Except for her hair the girl is pretty enough, and doesn't she keep your house right and tight? Maybe you don't want to lose your housekeeper!"

"No, no," said Ab Drem. "Housekeepers are nothing to find."

"As for your wife, Drem, may she rest in her grave. She died decently."

"Gossips have long memories," said Ab Drem, his chest hollow with the old pain. Still, his face bore a considering look. "Yet it's worth thinking on."

"Think fast, brother," said Ab Seroy. "You may be sure there are others thinking, too. These next days might be a time to speak to Harlan about, say, the brandy cellaring; and bring in the other matter while you have his attention."

"Humph," said Ab Drem. He turned his face back to War, but with such distraction that he forgot to spy at all and Ab Seroy, laughing, cut Ab Jerash to pieces.

"I'll see retribution, Seroy," said Ab Jerash cheerfully. "Right now I want tea. Wife! Wife! Or any one of those damned hens, where are they? Wife!"

"No tea for me," said Ab Drem, pushing back his stool. "When the nights are longer the days are shorter. Yet the day's work is the same."

"The longest night is soon past," said Ab Seroy, relighting his pipe. "See that you use it to think about what you will offer Harlan, and not to dream of men with whiskers like seals."

Ab Drem thought, It wasn't the whiskers bothered me. It was the eyes. "Good day, Seroy. Good day, Jerash, and thank you. I'm off."

"Away you go, then," said Ab Jerash, slapping Ab Drem on the back. "Dream not"—that was an Upslope blessing. "Or if you do dream, come back and I'll give you that same sedative and you shall sleep in the cedar bed. Tell your girl to make you camomile tea."

"Tell her not to make it for Ab Harlan's son," said Ab Seroy. "It doesn't suit for newlyweds."

Ab Drem rode the last miles home deep in thought, oblivious to the boniness of the mule.

6

"OH, SISTER," cried Dai. "What have you done?"

"What have I *done?*" Kat answered him furiously, crouching between her brother and the man sprawled on the white tiled hearth. "I found him on the beach. What do you want? It was right, right."

But everything was wrong.

It had begun to feel wrong as soon as she came into sight of Cliff Tooth House. Climbing the steep path from the sea, crossing the edge of morning forest sweet with balsam, there had been nothing to think about but the man's unwieldy balance and her own, and the work of walking. She dared not put him down. But the moment her feet had entered the familiar stony track that crossed the cliff top to the house, an ominous hesitation had begun to seep up through her as though from the place itself.

She refused to acknowledge it, yet it forced her to look fearfully for any sign of Dai or Ab Drem, and made her quick and clumsy at the latch. She pushed open the door gratefully with her knee; for her burden, as burdens will, had grown heavier the closer she came to laying it down. She eased him as lightly as she could from her back onto the hearth, and for a moment there had been nothing to feel but relief at having the weight gone. She crouched against the wood box, seeing stars.

Everything was wrong.

He sprawled awry across the white tiles that were spotless except for their dust of windblown ash. In that flawless room he looked disorderly and dark, his swollen arm flung out. He was smutty with sand and blood, and her sweater did not cover him. On the beach his nakedness had frightened her, yet there it had felt right, as a seal by its nakedness is clothed; in Ab Drem's house it was perverse and shocking, and she threw the brown cloak over his body. The nakedness of his unconscious face she could not cover. He was open and vulnerable in this place where she had always been so guarded, and she flinched from looking at him.

In her haste to help him she had forgotten his hurt leg; now she saw that a deep tear ran from just above the toes of his right foot halfway to the knee. Her gray skirt was soaked with his blood. She was drawn between the terror that he might have bled to death, and a revulsion for that blood. Though she had borne him sturdily up Horn Loft with his weight across her shoulders, here in her father's house she could scarcely bear to touch him. She tore a clumsy bandage from a cleaning rag and bound it, flinching, about his leg and foot.

An unnameable sense of familiarity stopped her. Small Gray, now indignant on the mantel with all four feet drawn up, had been a young cat once and a midnight hunter; his cold fur had carried an odor of night, wildness, speed. Kneeling over this man, Kat remembered it, for he smelled like that: like open doors, like a young cat come from hunting.

She did everything she could do without touching him. She stoked the dull coals with Ab Drem's meeting-day log. She changed her bloodstained skirt and shirt, which smelled of man. She washed her hands and found a kerchief for her hair.

It was as though she were becoming part of the clean house again. Angry and businesslike, she mopped up the splashes of blood between door and hearth. She stripped her sweater from him, reclaiming it. He was sprawled so crookedly on the hearth tiles; she would draw him to lie straight, at least, in case Ab Drem should come home and find his kitchen in disarray. Severely, she knelt to do so.

But he made a sound like a child's cry, and curled sideways as a fish does when it is thrown on the dock. He took a fold of her clean skirt in his fist; there were no words, but the tone had been clear enough: desolation, fear.

He would die.

Forgetting her clean skirt, she knelt over him. "Don't, don't!" she cried. "You're all right. You're all right."

Remembering how close the seals on the beach huddled with their mates and babies, she nudged her knees against him and fiercely patted his back. "You're all right."

It was at that moment that Dai, frumpy with hangover, had rambled through the door.

He stopped, stared. "What's this?" he cried. And then, "Oh, sister, what have you done?"

"What have I *done?*" Like a criminal caught she raged at him. "I found him on the beach. What do you want?" It was wrong for her to go to the beach. "It was right, right."

"On the beach?" said Dai blankly. "Found? . . ." He stepped closer, and saw. "*Oh.* My god, then. The beach!" Apologetically he bobbed his head to her. "Thought you had a . . . a man with you."

Outraged, Kat spat out Ab Drem's favorite profanity, unabridged.

He had not known she knew it. "Sister! I mean . . . He has no clothes on."

Because she would never call Dai by the names their father called him, she shook both fists at him. He backed away hastily, his mouth round like an O. When he could speak, he said, "That surf . . . Nobody could swim. . . ."

"See the marks of the rocks on him!"

"Then how did he get up . . . ?"

"I carried him. Dai! Dai!" And then she realized

that Dai's name sounded like the word she was afraid of, and said, "The doctor. You go, right now."

He made the word "doctor" with his mouth, soundlessly. At last he said, "Doctor. All right," in a tone of tremendous relief, and escaped out the door.

He would come back. Dai always came back.

The Rig had redoubled his blind grip on Kat's skirt. There was nothing to do but kneel and wait. Defending him to Dai had driven her subtly over some boundary of allegiance, so that she no longer sided with the house against the man, but with the man against the house. The price of it was that she, too, became a foreigner. Like him, she smelled of salt and animal and blood.

"You're all right," she told him vehemently. "You're all right."

The wind had stopped. The only sound was the fire rattling in the grate; it sank lower, and hushed. Small Gray jumped to the floor with a soft thud.

Dai came back. He came alone, panting, sidling through the door with his chin tucked in as though to ward off a rebuff.

"Doctor won't come," he gasped. "He's with Ab Harlan. Dyspepsia. Told me . . ."

"What."

"He said, 'No fear, can't kill a native.' "

Kat loosed the Rig's fingers from her skirt, as one would pick off a kitten, claw by claw; they closed again tightly on her hand. She said dully, "Ab Harlan eats too much."

Out of the long silence Dai said, "It's a Rigi, isn't it."

"Rig," she corrected him automatically. "That's how he said it: one Rig."

Shifting his feet in their heavy boots, Dai said, "Let me look."

She said angrily, "He's not some fish!"

"No," said Dai.

Sullenly she made room for him. His smell, too, was foreign to this house, a pleasant reek of hay and sweat. With slow hands he turned the Rig to and fro, as though he looked at flank and hoof. "Bad leg. He was tied up, see?" He showed her the marks of rope on ankle and wrist.

"No!"

"He was tied." He sat back, rubbing his face. "What shall we do?"

He had said, *We*. In that instant she loved him more than anything alive. Kat said lamely, " . . . He has to be washed."

"Thought about it," said Dai. "Coming along. Might get the cattle healer."

"He's not some cow!"

"Knew you wouldn't like it."

Kat bent over the man who curled around her knees. "All right, then," she said, her voice muffled. "That's a good idea, Dai."

Dai rose, looking happy. "Quick as can be," he said.

But he had scarcely turned to go when the door slammed, and a ghost of cold air stirred the house.

"What the devil is this?" said Ab Drem.

At the sound of Ab Drem's voice the man on the hearth flinched, and Kat jumped back away from

44

him. She had not intended to; her body did it for her. Dai stood frozen, his head drawn back into his shoulders. He always stood so in that house.

Ab Drem's boots rang on the flagstones.

"What the devil?" He was tall and tight under his broad black hat, and he did not like to bend down. He looked like a crane that peers with one eye and then the other. He saw that the man was naked. "What's this? What? Cover it! Not you." Kat, who had turned in alarm to replace the fallen cloak, halted in confusion. "You."

Dai stooped and did it for her.

Ab Drem would come no closer than he could touch with his riding stick. He held it out now, and it shook a little; he hesitated, withdrew. The man had flung out his brown arms, but his face was as shut as a book.

Ab Drem's face was rigid; but it was always rigid. Ominously he turned to Dai and said, "Tell." It did not occur to him that his daughter could have anything to do with it.

As always when he spoke to his father, Dai's mouth opened and shut twice before any sound came out. At last he tried, "Fisherman?" with a squeak.

"Fisherman!" Disdain soured Ab Drem's lean face. "Why, we're nowhere near the sea."

"Shipwreck . . ." Dai continued in a small voice, and gestured toward the cliffs.

The room seemed to be filling with a dark vapor, imperceptible at first and then slowly throttling, like smoke from a fireplace when the damper jams. With rising violence, Ab Drem, who knew everything already, told Dai's story for him.

"Fisherman. A dirty . . . Carried it up, did you? Why of all the mad . . . Driftwood is one thing, you brainless bolt, but this . . . in this condition . . . It's no business of ours, Dairois Mikrash, none. But what do you know of business? A fisherman! If you had to meddle with a native, why couldn't you drag it Downshore?"

Dai shook his head.

"Because you didn't think. You never think. God knows what vermin it may . . . They have their own witch doctors. Downshore."

As though to redeem himself, Dai said lamely, "Did . . . did think about the cattle healer . . ."

"One wise thought at least," said Ab Drem. "I cannot imagine why you would bring it here. A native! Naked as shame itself . . . Insulting your sister . . . Out to the byre with it! I have nothing against animals, but not in my house." His voice rose shrilly. "I will have no more natives in my house!"

He stopped with a gasp and looked about as though frightened by his own vehemence. Straightening his black hat, he said with dignity, "You have frightened the child."

Turning to Kat, his voice was kindly, almost sweet. "Don't fret, girlie." Possibly he was remembering that she used to cry over dead birds. "The dirtier, the tougher. Natives are like seals—to kill them you have to club them a good crack in the right place."

She flinched like a dog that hears a thunderclap.

To Dai, Ab Drem continued more calmly, "Sometimes I don't believe you have a mind at all. Now clear away the mess you have made."

He turned away; then he turned back.

"Right away, sir." Dai's words were mumbled, hardly intelligible.

But, as though against his will, Ab Drem came one step closer and bent his knees with a creak. Passing the stick to his left hand he reached out as if in a dream, and took the man's rough jaw in hand. He turned the young face to the firelight.

The man opened his eyes; they were clear and profoundly gray, like the sea where it is deepest. He looked long at Ab Drem, and moved his mouth to speak.

In an instant Ab Drem was on his feet again, wiping his hand on his trousers. "Get it out!" he cried. He turned with a clatter of boots, and did not hear as behind him the man made the same small desolate sound as before, curling up again, but this time around nothing.

Bending hastily, guiltily, Dai gathered him up in one clumsy gesture. "Byre," he mumbled to his sister. And as comfort, "Cattle healer."

But she, kneeling with her hands spread stiffly on her thighs, said nothing at all.

7

SHE HAD SWEPT the hearth, swept the floor,
brushed her father's jacket, mended the tear in his
gray trousers. She had begun the stew, washed the
dishes, mended the frayed place on the curtains. She
had set the sourdough to sponge, turned the cheese,
sewn up the rent in Dai's pillow where the feathers
trickled out. As the afternoon wore on, the wind
rose and rose, and moaned, and Dai did not come,
and Kat did not go to the byre.

All her life, Kat had tried to be invisible. As long
as she kept her mouth shut and the house spotless,

her father noticed her no more than he noticed the chair he sat in; she polished his boots and made his porridge, and when he had forgotten her she vanished.

But today she did not dare go out. She felt her wicked destination must be branded on her face. To go out of the house was to go to one place: to the man, the man, to go asking, "Is he alive? Is he still alive?"

And Dai did not come.

What made it worse was that Ab Drem seemed to notice her more than usual, and redoubled his demands on her.

First he had lain down in his shirt and trousers for a nap, and she thought she might slip out then if she were quick. But she could hear him tossing in his box bed, and shortly he rose and came back to the hearth, asking crossly for camomile tea. She fixed the tea and he retired again, demanding his old nightshirt, which she fetched. Yet still he rattled and tossed, and rose again even crosser wanting a rum toddy, and was angry because she had to ask him how to make it. When he went back to bed that time she did not even try to leave, but began numbly to stir the sourdough biscuits. Nor was he long. He rose again and washed his face, looking gray and old.

"Are you ill, father?" she asked him shyly.

He answered brusquely that he was not, and that she was to be about her work. He went to dress himself, and returning, set up his game of War, which he played left hand against right. She tried to be quiet; if she so much as thumped with the rolling pin he snapped at her. She concluded that he had a headache.

It was after that, when she turned around with floury hands, that she noticed how he was looking at her. It was a considering look, thorough and long, and it did not spare any part of her.

She had tried so long to be invisible; yet suddenly her father was looking at her as though she were solid as a heifer at the fair. She knew it was because of what she had done. She stood floured to the elbow, flushed to the roots of her red hair.

"Child," said Ab Drem at last, "how old are you?"

"Sixteen, sir." She began unobtrusively to back away.

"Sixteen." He rubbed his tired face. As though in agreement with an invisible counselor he said, "It is time you were married."

It occurred to her dimly that last night she had been wishing to be married. She said, "Sir," in her most noncommittal voice.

Ab Drem, who did not hold dialogues with women, repeated, "Time, good time. Come here."

"I'm dirty," she said instantly. She indicated her floury arms.

"No matter. Come here."

She stepped back into the firelight. Her father rose and surveyed her silently, without touching her. When he spoke, it was to himself: "Eh, she's of age."

As though he had resolved something, he grew even a little coy and said, "I'll find a man for you, eh? Eh?" But he looked deathly tired, and sat down again in his too-tall, straight-backed chair.

Kat stood unmoving on the hearth. She would be married. Her father would find a man; she would belong to that man, and wear his name. There would be another house, and babies, and other boots to polish, and another hearth to sweep, and other biscuits to bake, forever and ever, until she died.

Just like Auntie Jerash.

"Sir," Kat said instantly, "I must milk the cow."

"You're a good girl," said Ab Drem unexpectedly. "Go along then. Maybe I'll nap easier by the fire."

He stretched out his long legs heavily, one by one.

"Thank you, sir," said Kat. She hooked the milk bucket to the yoke, with one of the water buckets to balance it. "Excuse me, sir."

She was so quiet sliding out the door that the chain of the yoke scarcely rang, and Ab Drem did not lift his eyes from his stocking feet. She walked calmly seaward to the byre side of the house, where there were no windows; and when she was sure she was out of sight, she ran like the hare on the hill.

Dai had built the byre himself, with Kat helping to roll the heaviest rocks; to spare Ab Drem the detested cattle smell he had built it well away. Kat was still a stone's pitch from the door when she halted her clattering run with a jolt, the buckets swinging on their chains. She knew he was dead. The man was dead.

The day had grown gray and wintry blue, the sun just set. Dai would have lit the lantern—he always lit the lantern; but there was no sliver of light from the cracks in the byre door. The man was dead, and lay in there, and Dai had gone for the sexton.

But she could not turn around and go back to Ab Drem. After a little her feet carried her nearer simply because she had said she would milk the cow and the cow was, after all, in the byre. When she was within a yard or so of the door she heard a little human sound and stopped fearfully to listen.

It was Dai's voice, singing the cracked fragment of an old lullaby that their mother had sung to them, about a bear in a cave that has two cubs, one red and one brown. Kat was the red and Dai the brown. When their mother died—Dai had been nine—he had made Kat learn it even though it was in the Hill tongue that she could barely understand. Through his weeping he had slapped her until she got it right. But she had never heard him sing it after that.

She stepped to the door and pushed it open a little, whispering, "Dai!"

The singing stopped instantly, and Dai rose out of the shadows. "You came!"

"I couldn't come till now," said Kat. "I couldn't get away."

He drew the door a little further open and she stepped through it into the half-warm dark, setting down the yoke blindly where she stood. There was an odor of manure and hay, of man, of some stark medicinal stench as pitchy as a broken pine branch. Soon she could make out the black blur of the mule in his stall, the cow, Moss, lying down but fidgeting, and Dai's bearded face, ghostly over the jersey she had knit for him.

"Wants to get up and be milked," Dai was saying in a hoarse whisper. "Told her no. He lies warm with her. But he doesn't wake."

Kat stepped past the hill of Moss's body in the hushing straw. Covered with Dai's old brown blanket, the Rig lay curled like a calf against the cow's flank. His eyes in the pale blur of his face were shut, and he breathed so slightly that he might not have breathed at all.

She knelt down in the hay beside him, touching his hand. It was cool and still, like the perch that she brought from Downshore in her wicker basket.

Dai knelt, scratching the cow between the horns. "So, Mossy." His voice was urgent, troubled. "Healer can't come. There's cattle plague in Rake. Ran there, ran back; this Rig just the same, the good cow keeping him. You didn't come! Doctored him myself, a little. But sister—he doesn't wake."

"He's cold," she said, lifting the chill hand up to her cheek that was flushed with running. Turning to her brother she said fiercely, "Dairois Mikrash n'Ab Drem, you are the best man that ever was."

"Me?"

"Yes. All you have run, all you have done."

"Nothing," said Dai, turning his face away.

"He's cold." She held the Rig's hand against her mouth. "What shall I do? He's cold, cold."

"Lies against that good warm cow."

"Brother, will you make a light?"

Dai rose, and after the blink and stink of sulphur the lantern bloomed in his hands. "Didn't light it before," he said. "Thought he might lie easier in the dark."

The man's face was translucent under its scurf of beard, as though there were no blood in it. Dai showed her how he had splinted the wrist and bound the leg with rags from which rose the pitchy reek that stood in the air like a post.

"Cattle salve," he said. "But he bled too much."

Kat looked in desolation at the Rig's skinned shoulders and knees. "It's not the bleeding," she said bitterly. "It's all of it. It's Father."

Because she could not bear despair, she found refuge in anger. "You'd better not die," she said furiously to the man's closed face. "You'd better not." Remembering the seals, she snugged her thigh against him so that he was cosy between herself and Moss. "Don't you listen to that old man. Don't you dare die; I'll hate you. Don't you die!" She stroked him firmly, in a rage. "I'll keep you. I'll find some-place."

She looked around wildly as though she might see a place as safe as her mother's lap.

"Sister . . ."

She raised her head grimly. "You still know that song," she said. "Don't tell me you don't. I heard you. Sing it now."

54

Glaring, she began the old worn lullaby. After a moment Dai turned his face away and sang clumsily along with her.

> *Bear in the black rock,*
> *Bear's two children.*
> *My red cub, O!*
> *My brown cub, O!*

> *Warm in the black rock,*
> *Bear's two children.*
> *My red cub, O!*
> *My brown cub, O!*

That was what it meant; the only words Kat knew exactly were *ouma* for the mother bear and for the cubs *katim na* and *katim yao.* "Katim na, O! My red cub, O!" Singing, she forgot the man and remembered her mother: the rocking, the sad voice, and how she had sat on her mother's left thigh, with Dai awkward on her right.

> *My red cub, O!*
> *My brown cub, O!*

Looking down, she saw the man's eyes open in his guttered face.

"Bad dream," he whispered.

"Mister," was all she could say. "Mister!"

"Was it you who sang?"

"Yes!"

Dai sat still as a pillar in Moss's shadow.

In a voice of despair the Rig said, "But you had red hair!"

She pulled off the gray kerchief, and her short curls sprang up like fire in the lantern light.

"I did not dream it," he whispered. "Very strange, this side of the water."

The chime of Moss's bell as she turned her huge head startled his eyes away from Kat's face. With no breath left, he said, "What is that?"

"Cow," said Dai in a rusty croak.

The man made the word *cow* silently; aloud he added courteously, "Very warm, this cow."

Dai was pleased. "Good cow." As though he could not contain himself, he added, "No cows where you come from?"

"No."

But the Rig was weaker than he had been. He looked on Kat with an anchored gaze. She was afraid that, like a boat, he might drift back into the dark.

In Downshore, Auntie Jerash had said with scorn, the natives named their boats so that they might call them back across the water. "What's your name?" Kat asked him craftily; by that sorcery she would hold him.

"They took it."

"What?"

"My name," he said. "They took it when they killed me."

"Killed you!"

"The elders," he said patiently. "They took my skin, my name. I am dead."

In superstitious horror she nearly dropped his hand; but she could feel the dull living pulse at his thumb. "They can't take your *name,*" she said. "It's a *name.*"

"They took it."

"Why would they want it?"

"*They* did not want it." With tired hope he said, "Maybe a new one comes."

He lay looking at her quietly. He was not like a boat at all but like water: He had tumbled through the rocks and up onto the shore, and like water he would sigh back into the darkness. There was no name for that but wave; there was nothing to hold.

"It was a wave I thought of," she said suddenly, as though if she made her fear clear she could fight it. "It comes up on the beach like you, a long wave, but then it turns and goes back." She held his hand tightly. "Don't, don't go back."

She thought for a moment that Dai had turned up the wick of the lamp; but it was the Rig smiling, his bleak face alight.

"Nall," he said.

"What?"

"Nall. That is my name."

"The name they took?"

"No. My new name. One comes, I said."

"Nall?"

"Long Wave. It means Long Wave." He closed his eyes.

"Nall," she said, in a panic to keep him. From his lips the word was a wave, a long sigh. She was sure it was not right to fish out a name like that and put it on. It was your father who named you. Still it was the only thing she had to hold him. "Nall, Nall."

He opened his eyes. "I will not die," he said harshly, and shut them again. But his hand was slack.

"What shall we do?" said Kat desperately, sitting back on her heels.

"Milk the cow."

"Milk the *cow*!"

But Dai urged Moss cautiously to standing and set one bucket to serve as a stool while he milked into the other. Over the rattle and hiss of the milk he spoke into Moss's flank. "Let the night darken a little, to hide me from the gossips. I'll take him inland. Doctor next to the tavern is good with bangs and bones."

"You can't take him inland," said Kat positively. He was a seal. What would the inland farmers know about a seal? "He'll die."

But here in the byre . . . Her hope rose like a fever. "I'll keep him here," she stammered. "Father never comes. Moss can keep him warm. I'll slip out when Father's gone, I'll wash him. The healer will come back from the cattle plague and see to him." Small Gray was too old; she would keep Nall instead. He would be her secret. Like the song, and then she would have somebody of her own. Like Moss for Dai, Nall for . . .

"No," she said aloud, horrified at herself. "He's not a *pet*!"

"Uh?" Dai stared, turning his forehead on Moss's belly.

"He has to go Downshore," said Kat, bright with shame. "Here is not where he goes. He has to be near the sea."

"*Down*shore," said Dai. "A fool goes Downshore in the dark. Before the Long Night? There are stories . . ." He shrugged. "Anyway, don't know a soul in Downshore."

"I do," said Kat suddenly. "I know an herb woman, from the market. She gave me an apple once. Mailin." That name came back to her, dimly; she thought it must belong to the rosy old woman. "Mailin, the best there is."

"You know where she lives?"

"Near the market," said Kat vaguely. "Everybody . . . Oh, everybody knows her. She keeps the herb stall."

"How do you know so much of Downshore, sister?" said Dai, troubled. "Don't know that it's decent."

Kat cast him a look of such scorn that he gazed down hastily into the milk bucket.

"A Rig would belong there," she said. "If they want money I'll . . . well. I'll get money some way."

Dai said to his hands, "You can have the milk money if you want."

"Oh, Dai!"

"It's fair," he said roughly. "You help milk."

She said nothing, only looked at him. Scowling, he said, "So. Come dark I'll take him. Downshore, by the cattle path, and nobody will see." He turned to face her and set both hands on his knees. "Sister," he said with his rare sweet smile, "I should have drowned you when you were little."

She returned his smile timidly and bent over Nall, but he was drifting out of reach. In an hour he would be farther away, down the cattle path to Mailin.

"There are market days," she said aloud. To hide her eyes from Dai, she bent over Nall and put her hand on the slow pulse at his neck. "I could ask for Mailin on a market day."

She rose and covered her hair. Dai brought a bucket half full of rainwater to balance the milk pail, hitched the yoke for her, and held it patiently at shoulder height.

"Nall," said Kat.

A quirk of the muscles around his mouth was all.

Turning blindly, she shouldered the yoke and stepped into the night. There was enough wind to raise tears on anybody; she had to stand for a moment in the middle of the yard with her face crooked in her sleeve, trying not to spill the milk. Then, with one long breath to be steady, she crossed to Cliff Tooth House and kicked open the latch.

Ab Drem stood scowling in his boots and greatcoat, putting on his hat.

"You've been none so quick," he snapped. "I've had to ready myself, in my own house. I won't have it." His face was etched with illness and annoyance. "I'm gone for the night," he said, "to Graystone's

60

cedar bed, to rid me of these damnable dreams. I'm
walking, for my health. Tell your brother to bring
the mule in the morning. And you, girlie"—he tied
the laces of his broad hat under his chin—"if I catch
you kicking that latch again I'll cane you. What
would your husband think?"

He left, slamming the door.

She walked to the hearth and set down the yoke
with a rattle.

Standing in the very middle of the flagstones she
counted carefully to one hundred.

Then, aloud in the empty house, she said his
name: "Nall." And still Ab Drem did not come back.
"Nall, Nall."

She turned on her heel.

"Father's gone," Kat gasped to Dai in the byre,
tying her cloak. "I'm coming with you."

8

THEY WENT DOWN without light, for Dai would
not have the lantern. The fingerling moon had not
yet risen, and they had to go by feel, Kat walking
ahead because she was not the one laden. Dai carried
Nall, rolled in his old blanket. When Kat looked
back at a turning of the trail she could see her
brother's bearded face, a knot of worry, and Nall's,
darker and smoother and scarred.

Upslope's distant outbuildings rose like ax blades
against the dim sky, jutting rigidly as though they
detested the earth they stood on. Sunk into the turf
by generations of slow hooves, the cattle path

skirted them as an ant trail skirts a fallen brick, dropping downward and away.

Feeling her way ahead with quick, short steps, Kat knew the land was changing because the sparse bracken of the cliff crest faded from the trailside and in its place rose heavy grass that brushed her boots with wet. All visible shapes grew rounder, as though aeons of dust from the slow erosion of those heights had sifted and settled on the fields below.

The dark grew soft. There were not many Downshore houses near the path, but here and there a low stone barn swelled from the turfy slope. Their irregular shapes were hard to know from bush or fallen stone. There seemed to be nobody about; here and there a farm dog dashed out gallantly to bark from a boundary wall, but no human followed. There were no voices, and from the thick-glassed windows no faint gleam. They passed downward, jolting their knees on abandoned earth.

Kat's nose, too, told her they were dropping into Downshore. Upslope had no smell, for the wind snatched it all away—but Downshore! Kat and Dai stumbled through the ticklish honey smell of hay; the chill, earthy tang of vineyards; wood smoke; manure; laundry that smelled like wind; the reek of caged rabbits; cool gardens half cabbage and half flowers; bread; garbage; pine tar; and, as lower and lower they trudged, the faint breath of the sea.

Dai stopped at a low stone stile to get his breath. "Ar!" he said, mopping his face. "Don't believe you carried him up the Loft!"

He stared at the lightless clutter of thatch beyond

the stile. "See how those walls lean! Built by uncles, every one, and guessing at the measure."

Kat bit her tongue; Dai had built the first byre himself, all of wood, and it had immediately blown down with him inside it. She looked anxiously at Nall; his face was stone.

"Hup," said Dai. He did not like stopping so near to houses. Staggering from the wall he found the track again, jerking a last glance over his shoulder. "Hoarding wood," he said. Most of the houses had a huge pile of driftwood stacked under a corner of the thatch or heaped in the yard under an old sail. "They'll burn it all for Long Night. The Year Fire."

"All of it?"

"Waste," said Dai, having no breath for more.

Since Kat could not reach Nall's hand, she held his unbandaged foot as they scuttled from shadow to shadow like mice.

"Everybody's off somewhere," said Dai. "Don't like it." When Kat did not answer he added nervously, "There's stories about Long Night week, in the dark."

There began to be more houses, close together, and the cattle path became a road. Dai halted uneasily in the black lee of a haystack. "Sister," he said, "what is that?"

Kat stood motionless, half in, half out of shadow. Nothing moved; yet something thrummed, less sound than vibration, shaking foot and thigh.

Without thinking, Kat laid the cool, sandy sole of Nall's foot against her cheek. "It's drums," she said.

The sound was like a hand that shakes a sleeper's shoulder. It was her body that woke. She stood

64

listening with her legs, as crickets do. Without knowing how she knew, she said confidently, "Everybody's down there. It's almost Long Night and they are waking up the drums."

"Do we have to go there?" Dai's voice was unexpectedly like a child's, desperate. "Do we have to?"

"I have to get Mailin," said Kat. "You can wait here if you want."

"No," said Dai with a groan. "Alone's no good." And he lurched out grimly into the road.

They walked more slowly now, wary as rabbits in a midnight garden. The further they walked, the louder swelled the drum. It was not the single clean beat that Kat remembered from the long-ago market, but a low, hairy throb of many drums together, muffled as though the sticks had been rolled in cloth. As they drew up to the edge of the town proper, the road became an alley and the sound shook the very stones. Dai sank back into the dark arch of a travelers' rest with Nall in his arms.

"I can't!" he sobbed. He put his face down on the familiar scratchy blanket. "It's clods falling on a coffin lid. I can't! Some demon makes that sound!"

Wonderingly, Kat said, "It's just drums."

"It's death," he sobbed. "It's our mother."

She did not understand him. Then she remembered it: the black crash of earth on the hollow wood, a dull sound, dulling, duller, until it was only the sound of dirt on dirt. "Oh, Dai!" she said.

She had not touched her brother that she could remember, not since their mother died; but now she huddled his head against her neck, one arm across his shoulder, the other around Nall so that she made a warm roof over them both with her body.

Looking down she saw Nall's eyelids flicker.

He spoke one word in a foreign tongue; then, "Drums!" he said. "The Snake!"

"Snake!" She drew up instinctively and glanced about.

The ghost of that first mischief crossed Nall's face. He whispered, "No snakes where you come from?" and then added, "They are dancing it," as though that were obvious.

Dancing the Snake. Kat thought of vipers, fat and black. "Nobody dances anything where I come from. Nall." She had his name now. "I'm bringing a healer for you. I have to go in there, where the drums are. The Snake—is it safe? Tell my brother it's safe."

Nall said only, "There is some safe place?" whether in hope or mockery she could not tell. His eyes were shut. Dai whined, burrowing his face into the blanket.

"I'm going," Kat said, rising.

From the shadows Nall's voice said forcefully, "Red hair!" and she halted. His eyes looked light-colored in the dark. He said, "You are more wonderful than the sun."

She stood wordless. Then, as though in a dream, she pointed to Dai and said, "You keep him company. It scares him."

Dai did not move, his face still hidden. As Kat slipped away, pulling her dark hood securely forward, she saw Nall gather his strength like a runner, and raise his good hand gently to touch Dai's cheek.

9

ENTERING THE DARK ALLEY was like entering a cleft in soft rock that has weathered round. Kat went forward by touch, laying her hand first against stucco, then against sandy stone.

In the narrow street, the sound was like a river, pushing at the walls and swelling to be so huge that it had distinguishable parts: There was the gray boom of the beat, with an occasional bright clack when a stick hit a drum rim; but there was also a low, hushing scuffle like scales on stone, and the moan of innumerable voices halfway between tune and hiss, or tune and sigh.

Kat thought of a great barbelled serpent, many-headed, many-voiced. Alive with curiosity and fear, she walked forward, and at a little turning the alley debouched with her into the marketplace.

She had expected the diabolical; what she saw were the packed backs of a silent crowd. Men were hatless, women wore long cloaks like her own. Two small girls squatted at the curb playing Scissors Paper Stone. Kat hung, thwarted like a down-bound fish that comes up against a dam. The crowd was rapt and still. Here and there a woman wept quietly. All were strangers—the apple woman was not there. Kat opened her mouth to ask of anyone, "Please, where is Mailin?" but fear closed it again. The drum boomed; she could scarcely think; she whispered to hear her own voice: "The herb stalls. Beyond the portals."

Taking the hood of her cloak firmly in one fist, she turned sideways and slipped into the crowd.

Shoulders and backs and hips jostled her on many levels; the crowd smelled of bodies and babies and damp wool. Feet shifted to make room for her feet, and elbows lifted to let her pass. A moment or two of determined squirming and she popped out again into the open. With the tail of her cloak still trapped between a fat man and his fat wife, she stood in the front ranks of a broad circle.

There were many drums. Their dull, fleshy beat surged over something that moved in the middle of the square, breaking around it like a wave.

"There's the Snake," thought Kat. "The Snake!"

A pace or two away roiled a long coil of men and

women in their common clothes, locked shoulder to shoulder and hand to hand. They moved together in a slow shuffle to the thud of the drum. Step, step, step, pause, back, back. Their heads were bowed. As they danced they sang, if it could be called singing. It was a wordless, minor moan.

The drums shook the earth, they shook Kat's bones. She had forgotten Mailin, almost forgotten Nall.

Around her the crowd jostled gently, and the line of dancers traded off here and there. A girl a little older than Kat backed out of the line of bent bodies, which healed instantly behind her, and returned to the crowd to lift a baby from a young man's hip. He gave up the child without a word and walked forward to the line; at his light touch it opened, gathered him in, and instantly was whole. The Snake danced on.

Kat thought, "I could do that. Go up and touch, like that, one touch, they let me in . . ."

She put one foot forward.

A hand brushed her shoulder. She turned half around. The girl with the baby was whispering, "Blessing! What are you doing here?"

"Me?" Kat gaped stupidly.

"I've frightened you," said the other, hitching the baby higher on her hip. "I'm Suni. I sell you a perch every market day."

Every market day . . . But Kat had never raised her head to look.

Suni turned the child's face as introduction, saying matter-of-factly, "I thought you might remember the baby. Why have you come? No one from Upslope ever comes to the Snake."

"Mailin," said Kat immediately, snatching Suni's arm. "I came for Mailin."

The girl stood abruptly straight, as though Mailin were the most reasonable person in the world to ask for. "Shall I fetch her?"

"Oh, please!"

"She's dancing," said Suni. "Take Rosie, then." She hefted the child into Kat's arms and went seeking along the coil of dancers like a dog sniffing at a line of ankles. She vanished.

Kat held Rosie awkwardly. She had held her young cousins, but they did not bounce as much as this round-faced child. The baby arched her back and squealed.

"Now, Rosie," said Kat, trying to get a firm grip on her through her sweaters. "Be good now, there's a Rosie."

Rosie flapped her arms, squirreling herself around in her jersey. Kat forgot about the Snake and was wondering desperately whether to grab the child's hair and haul her back square the way she had hauled Nall into her old brown sweater, when Suni came back and said, "Here's Mailin!"

It was not the apple woman.

Kat looked up expecting to see a dear bent bustling lady with basket and shawl. Instead her gaze rose to man height to meet eyes like brook water in a dark lean face. The woman was broad in shoulder and hip; her dark hair was gathered into a bundle at her neck. Starlight and sweat gleamed on the sinews of her wrists, on her cheekbones, on the hook of her flared nose.

"I am Mailin," she said in a deep voice.

Poor Kat. At the end of an endless day, she had expected a biddy hen and had met an eagle. Rosie bounced, and Kat's hood fell back.

"I found a Rig on the beach," she said clearly.

Mailin said, "Ah!"

"He's out there," said Kat. "You'd better help him." And she burst into tears.

To be crying, in the middle of the marketplace in front of all the strangers in the world, and not to be able to stop. To be led blind and stumbling through the parting crowd, to be sat down on a strange dark doorstep with her face on her knees. When she raised her head at last she was not done crying, but she had spent enough of it to pack the rest forcibly away. She drew a sharp, hard breath.

"That was well wept," said Mailin. "Someday may you weep the rest of it."

Kat turned her wet face in apprehension, but Mailin added seriously, "That you may not go so burdened." In Mailin's lap Rosie sat perfectly still, and when Kat looked at her she smiled her plain baby smile. Mailin's smile was grave and complex, in a net of wrinkles and bones. She said, "Does your breath belong to you again?"

Kat nodded, although it did not. Mailin spoke over the drums. "Shall we go to this Rig right now, or is there anything I must know first?"

Kat had never been asked anything respectfully in her life. She had never been asked anything at all, except why she had not done this or that. She looked over her shoulder to see who Mailin spoke to, but Suni was gone. The eagle woman had asked her, Kat, what was needed as seriously as if she had been a man.

When Kat spoke it was from some part of herself that had never stirred before, and which had nothing to do with Nall. She asked urgently, "Do they dance that every year?"

Mailin's smile deepened slightly, raising the scything lines at the corners of her eyes. "Every year. Every single year it will be here for you to dance."

"Then let's go to him right now," said Kat.

Mailin rose with the baby on her hip as though she had carried many. "Suni has gone for light. She will meet us at the turning. One may not bring light into the center when the Snake is danced. Where have you left him?"

"At the end of the alley," said Kat. "There was a place to sit down." She had to skip to keep up, for Mailin's stride was long.

The woman looked over her shoulder. "He is hurt?"

Again she spoke with grim respect, as to an equal.

"His arm," said Kat. "And his leg." After a moment she offered what seemed most important: "They took away his skin."

"Ah!" said Mailin. "They do that."

Kat said nothing. The two walked in silence, except that Mailin looked back once with her eagle

72

face, and something in it made Kat skip twice and touch her sleeve.

"Ma'am."

Mailin said nothing, but slowed.

"He keeps trying to come to a safe place."

"Ah!" said Mailin. "He came to you?"

Disconcerted, Kat fell back a pace, watching Mailin's ankles. Suni joined them, coming around a jumble of piled driftwood with a little yellow lamp bobbing in one hand. In that world of strangers she looked known and beloved. She took Kat's hand, and together they led Mailin down the crooked alley, the drums fading and muting, becoming again a heavy thud, like earth falling on a coffin lid.

"Everybody cries at the Snake, Lali," Suni was saying, calling Kat by the Downshore word for sister. "The Snake is danced for the dead, to remember them and let them go. Then we are ready for Long Night. Don't be ashamed."

"That dance wasn't like dying," Kat said suddenly. "It was like the bottom part of being alive."

Mailin's low laugh rang from the dark behind them. "That is what it is, Lali," she said. "That is what it is!"

As they neared the end of the alley, Kat dropped Suni's hand and darted ahead. "My brother," she said. "He's afraid. Dai! Oh, Dai!"

There was a jerking movement in the black arch of the travelers' rest. Yellow lantern light fell on Dai's face, openmouthed and greased with terror; he held Nall's face to his shoulder, hidden in the blanket.

"No," said Kat, stumbling to her knees beside them. "He hasn't! He said he wouldn't! No!"

"Breathes all right," gasped Dai.

He clutched Nall. From some separate corner of herself Kat saw what he was seeing: demons of the drum, their faces lit by fire. The one with the beak nose stooped upon him slowly, like a vulture. She handed a heavy bundle to the one with the lamp, and the bundle squealed and writhed.

"Oh, Rosie," said the lamp demon, adding apologetically to Kat, "She's teething."

"He's not dead," Kat was repeating. "He's not dead."

Mailin knelt, but instead of looking at Nall she looked at Dai.

He gazed straight back, forgetting to duck his head. Even though she had not asked, he said suddenly, shyly, "I'm Dai. Her brother."

"Dai," she said. "I am Mailin. You are a brave man."

"Me?" Like Kat he looked over his shoulder, but there was nobody else.

"Do the men of Upslope come to dance the Snake? No. They are as afraid as you are. Yet you have not run away."

She had lifted the blanket from Nall's empty face. She looked him over from neck to foot, as a cow licks her calf from nose to tail to see that it is whole.

Sharply she asked, "Who bandaged his leg and hand?"

"Wasn't supposed to be nothing," said Dai, morti-
fied. "Nobody to call . . ."

"It was you?" Mailin's brilliant eyes were on him.
"I could have done no better."

He pulled in his head like a turtle. "Nothing.
Cattlesalve."

"You are a doctor?"

"No!" In confusion he looked at his hands; patting
Nall's cheek clumsily, he asked, "Will he be all
right?"

"Give him to me."

"Weighs a bit," said Dai, but she had lifted Nall
smoothly from him, and he was sitting on cold stone
with an empty lap. "Ar!" Dai muttered, awestruck.
"She could lift a calf!"

"You have done well to carry him so far."

"It was her that carried him. Up Horn Loft, by
herself." Dai waved his hand toward Kat, who stood
a little aside from them looking at Nall and Mailin
with a pinched face. Dai added hastily, "But she's
decent. Even if she's strong. My sister." And in a
hoarse aside to Kat, "You all right?"

"Yes," said Kat, looking away. "She's got him
now."

"Has she!" he said in a passionate whisper. "She's
a good one! She'll mend him all right."

"We'd better go." Kat was looking at her feet.
Next to Mailin she seemed very small and young
and empty-handed. "He is where he goes," she said
in a louder voice. "We'd better."

"He is not where he goes," said Mailin. "Neither

are you." When Kat raised her head the older woman added, "He came to you."

"To me?"

"Did you not call him?"

Kat stood with her mouth open.

"Will you come to my house?" said Mailin, but Kat, as though rooted, did not move.

"Ch-h-h!" Dai told her. "Stand staring while the man freezes to death. Keeping this lady from her work. She says come along and you'll come, sister, or I'll carry you."

To Mailin Kat said suddenly, "My name is Kat."

"Only a little farther, Lali Kat." Mailin smiled and turned away, the dark shape of Nall's body making her shoulders look broader. Suni led, with Rosie and the lamp. Unexpectedly, Dai took Kat's hand in his big rough one.

"Hup," he said, and she came with him. "Besides," he added as they followed the bobbing light, "she's got my good blanket."

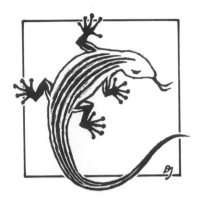

10

THEY DID NOT GO back through the Snake. They skirted the town, past pigsties and deserted middens, then turned south toward Horn Loft along the shore. The only beach Kat knew was Nall's, where the western sea roiled among the fallen stones, but here Horn Loft was like an arm that warded off the ocean's blows, holding Downshore's harbor in its elbow's crook. The low combers curled and flattened, white ghostly lines on the black water. A low, mumbling, repeated sigh rose from them like a chorus in round. Stumbling beside Dai through the slippery beach grass she thought, This is some other, stiller sea.

The beachward dwellings were a shapeless jumble, strung along the path where the black cliffs began to rise out of the sand. The backs of the houses were dug into the earth, and their fronts faced the bay on posts, like badgers at the mouths of burrows. From their steep shingles fluttered strings of tattered white flags stamped with some faded symbol; in the dark these looked like flocks of sea birds rising in lines—pelicans, or geese.

One house had light.

"Here." Mailin turned abruptly left, up a flight of worn and hollow-sounding steps. Suni jumped ahead with the lantern, and its swinging beam made a jagged scatter of the stairs, which rose over the pilings to a looming verandah that boomed under Mailin's feet. To Kat it seemed like one more cliff for climbing, one more Horn Loft.

From under the cavernous dark porch piles came a frightening slight movement, but a familiar smell.

"A cow!" said Dai.

As Kat pulled herself up the last step, a door opened to firelight half blocked by a man's body.

He was tall and broad, like Horn Loft against a heavy sky. Kat stopped, stared: part of the bulk was beard, and part was a young otter that crouched on his shoulder like a cat. Aside from his beard the man was bald, and big, even discounting the otter. He was eating a buttered muffin, and the air was sleepy with the smell of baking. Kat ached; she had hardly eaten all day long.

"Here's that Rosie," said the man, taking the baby from Suni and giving the child the rest of the muffin. He laid his big hand over Mailin's on Nall's shoulder. "Mailin, who is this?"

"Pao—a Rig has come."

"A Rig!" Pao's grin had a gappy place left by missing teeth, like a horse's. He looked at Kat and Dai with admiration. "To you he came?"

Mailin strode ahead to the farther room, from which the firelight shone. Timidly Kat began to follow, but stopped with a squeak. In the lamplight she had seen an enormous tortoise row slowly off across the bare floorboards, and a bull snake slide around a battered shovel by the fireless hearth.

"They live in here because the kitchen is too hot for them," Pao said reasonably. He slapped his leg. "I cannot dance the Snake any more, so the snakes come dance with me."

Smiling, he limped after Mailin through the fire-lit door, his right leg stiff at the knee.

"Pao heals animals," said Suni, following him with the lamp. The first room was doused in dark again, but Kat held the glimpse of it on the back of her eye: pale wide walls, black beams; the tortoise motionless in the middle of the striped hearth rug; a green lizard clinging to the door frame like a sculpture of itself. And stretched above the hearth was a gray sealskin, sewn with red and silver; she saw its whiskers, its empty eyes.

Kat followed Suni into the kitchen, and stood blinking.

She was used to the hearths of Upslope that were

polished, correct, cold. But this kitchen was clay-hearthed, oiled with generations of smoke; dried herbs hung in pungent bunches from the beams, and the walls wore a friendly clutter of oilskins, hatchets, striped rugs. A dog-fox yapped from underneath a bench. Perched on a hoe handle, a parrot scratched its ear.

On the scrubbed boards in the middle of the room Mailin stood patient and motionless, as though Nall's weight were nothing—as though what Kat could have offered Nall were nothing, meager and cold. Surrounded by this warmth and plenty, Kat thought: I couldn't give him anything at all.

The thought was so far beyond pain that she had to stand absolutely still in order not to feel it, and look indifferently at a box on the hearth that held a wary mother cat and six gray kittens.

"Get along," said Pao, setting the otter afoot. It darted under the bench, hissing at the fox. Giving Rosie to her mother, Pao shifted the box of cats and from a tall cupboard pulled a rolled pallet covered with striped cotton, which he tossed down open across the hearth. Muttering, the parrot dislodged itself from the hoe and rolled into the next room with its sailor's gait. Pao threw down a coarse clean sheet.

"Help me, Lali Kat," said Mailin.

Kat opened her mouth to say, "I can't," because all her help seemed worthless, but her traitor feet walked her forward. She did say sullenly, "He's too heavy," to which Mailin replied, "We are two."

It was bear him or drop him. Kat had to look at

his face then; in this comfortable bright room he looked broken, not like a person but like a rabbit's carcass, a heap of dirty clothes. Yet she knelt beside him and laid her hand on his neck.

"I'll be gone," said Suni, understanding at once. "Back to the dancing, and my man."

"People will ask questions," said Mailin. "Answer them. But no visits. This is not finished."

Suni nodded. Laden with baby and lamp, she kissed Kat's cheek. "A Rig brings luck, if he lives," she said. "Or storms. But you're a strong woman." The curtain swung behind her as she left.

Dai stood stiffly in the middle of the room. "My sister," he said quickly, as though he too might be asked to go. "I won't leave her."

"I'm fine," said Kat, who was not.

"You shall not leave her," Mailin said to Dai, "but in this house there is always other doctoring." As if to demonstrate her words, the dog-fox hopped from the bench into the shadows: It had only three legs. "Do you know anything about cracked udders?"

"Bear's fat!" said Dai instantly.

"Ah!" Pao cast him a sharp look. "A healer? The black cow under the verandah—nothing eases her at all."

He whistled on a rising note; the otter dashed from underneath the couch and he took it up, swinging his stiff leg with a gait like the parrot's.

Dai followed him. "That Mailin will mend your Rig," he said comfortably to his sister. "If you need me, I'll be with the cow."

The kitchen was full of the sound of the sea. Mailin brought blankets, salves, and a clay hot-water jug; under the floorboards a muffled murmur and thump told of the men busy with the cow. Kat's hands gripped each other in her lap. Nall was Mailin's now, not hers. Nothing was hers.

But he did not warm, and he did not wake.

At last Mailin said, "So," and sat back on her heels. Her face was thoughtful, stern. "So it is," she said.

Kat stared at her from the shadows, huge-eyed with a rising fear.

Mailin pushed the hair from her eyes. "It is your turn, Lali Kat."

"My turn?"

"This man needs you."

"Needs me?"

"Yes."

Nall on the pallet looked like something the tide had finished with and pushed away—flotsam among uprooted kelp and legless crab shells.

"He came to you."

"He did not! I just found . . ."

Mailin rose and opened her empty hands. "I have done all I can."

Kat cried, "No!" and sprang forward to Nall's shoulder. "You're the healer!" she cried to Mailin. "Heal him!" When Mailin said nothing she gasped, "You'd let him die? Oh, you would! You would! You're old, like Father, you don't care!"

She snatched up Nall's hand against her chest, as though by warming it she could warm all of him. "I'll take him back! I can carry him. I carried him before!"

"Lali Kat," said Mailin.

Kat turned her face away, and hunched her body, like a shield, between Mailin and Nall.

"He came to you," said Mailin. "Did you call?"

"Call?" Something in the quiet voice stilled her and she stayed kneeling, looking down at Nall. She heard fire, surf, and his slow breathing: bitterly slow, a decision every breath, a long wave rising up and pausing, falling, withdrawing. She remembered her own voice on the beach shouting what she had sung silently for years of barren hearth and cold bed: *Come to me!*

"It's true," she said aloud. "I called him."

"He has come." Mailin's voice was soft. "What does he need now, to stay?"

"He needs to know somebody wants him." The words leaped from her. "My father hates him. My father hates *me*. . . . Oh, my father! Nall!"

She lifted him—filthy, ugly, cold—to hold him between her breasts and her updrawn knees. "I don't care if you're a beast," she cried, to him only. "I don't care what you are. You're the same as me. The same as me!"

She heard the drum of her own heart, and of his; she heard the surf and the crackle of flame. The burning wood was cedar, and smelled like the cleft of forest on the path to the beach.

Kat cried. She cried all the tears unwept before, for weariness and Nall dying and this endless day; yet more than that for the baby with a bear's face, for the clods on her mother's coffin, for lonely evenings and lonely mornings, the yoke, the bare dusty hearth. She cried for her shorn red hair. She cried beyond crying, blind, into a place where there was room to breathe; and when she stopped crying she was clean.

Someone spoke softly.

Over the emptiness of having wept out everything at last, she heard him without surprise, looked down to see his face dazed, inhabited.

He labored toward her until he came into her language, and he said, "On every shore. You."

"Nall," she said.

Her heart was so huge with homecoming that surely he could feel it hurl itself against him, surf on a steep beach. His hand lay over it.

"What is your name?" He was spent, urgent.

"Kat."

"Kat!" The corners of his mouth curled up over the broken canine; he was beautiful, beautiful. "Cats where I come from," he whispered, alive with mischief. "They are warm, like cow." And he laughed.

It was not so much later when Mailin rose, quietly, from her knees. She gathered up the old cow blanket and spread it cautiously over Kat, who had fallen asleep with her cheek on Nall's forehead. Nall slept with his fist closed firmly on the collar of Kat's shirt, and Mailin tucked the ends of the blanket around him, too.

From beneath the floorboards rose a disconsolate and fussy mooing.

"Ah!" said Mailin with satisfaction. "I might at least be helpful with the cow."

II

KAT WAS FIVE YEARS OLD. Beyond her closed eyelids was not the stuffy blackness, winter and summer,
of the box bed, but peach-colored light, frail and
cool. A low sighing went on and on, and with it
another sighing that was muffled, mysterious, far
away. She was five years old and her back was
settled into the curve of her mother's sleeping body.
Her mother's arm lay over her, and her slow breath
was part of that tidal sigh.

"Ma," said Kat, and woke herself.

She was not five, and it was not her mother's
body that she lay curled against in her wrinkled

clothes, but Nall's. It was his sleeping breath she heard, mixed with the voice of the sea, and his warm arm lay over her. He smelled of cattle salve and otter and man. The strange room before her face was pale gold with morning rising, and a small fire snapped in the grate.

The parrot blinked at her from the hoe handle; otherwise the room was empty.

Kat lay still as a mouse trapped in cupped hands.

She was embraced, in a strange house in a strange dawn, with sighing and the musk of man all about her. The length of her back, the backs of her knees, were pressed motionless against another body.

She tried to make herself small, to draw herself fearfully from beneath that weight and warmth; but the one who held her made a squeak of protest and in his sleep settled his arm more firmly over her.

Somewhere outside the house rose a man's voice, singing.

Out of the sea's grip, hup!
I have drawn my heart.
Out of those dark arms, hey!
I have coaxed my boat . . .

Kat lifted Nall's arm and rolled free, her heart hammering; but he only made the same annoyed chirp as before, curled tighter, and slept on.

She looked at him from a safe distance. In the mixed light of fire and morning he seemed no longer like a dark wave ebbing. He was utterly earthly, ruddy as a duckling in the sun. Dry, his brown hair stood up thick and harsh, and he slept as furiously as a runner runs. His good hand was curled into a fist.

After a moment she slid back shyly and covered up his bare shoulder with the old blanket that smelled of cow.

Last night came back in pieces. Where was Dai? She knew he would not have left her if it were not all right, but nothing felt real at all, except for Nall in the determination of his sleep. She rose and found her way timidly onto the verandah, hugging herself.

The sun had come over the cliff's edge and was burning away the mist in veils of pewter and peach and gold; in the calm harbor the water was blue where it deepened. The tide was out. She could smell wood smoke and fish. Distantly she heard children shouting; a dog barked.

Mailin was striding back along the beach path, followed by a cloud of gulls.

She had a yoke across her shoulders, with two wooden buckets swinging from it. Kat stared, as though she saw herself. Mailin climbed the broad loud steps and set the buckets down with a rattle.

"Springwater, Lali Kat. The gulls want it to be clams."

"He's still asleep," Kat whispered, reproach stronger than shyness. There were no known rules to follow; she felt stiff and askew, and awkwardly smoothed her hair.

"Nor shall he wake for a while, no matter how we shout. No one can sleep like the Rigi, and that one has come far." Mailin smiled, waking all the wrinkles around her eyes. "As have you."

In the morning light she looked quite ordinary. There was gray through her hair like frost, and her brown forearms were as thick as a man's. Kat looked at her own wrists, which were sturdy from work, and felt obscurely pleased.

"Dai has gone home to milk the cow. I am to tell you that he will come back for you soon, and that he will see there is no problem with your father." Mailin shifted the buckets into the shade and picked up the mother cat, who had come out stiff-legged and waving her tail.

"This is Beck." Mailin gave her the cat to hold. "Are you hungry?"

"Oh, yes!" said Kat, suddenly aware that she had scarcely eaten since the day before yesterday. Beck mewed; Kat put her down and she ran back inside to her kittens, her tail straight up.

Mailin laughed. "Come, then!"

But Kat paused on the verandah, listening to the sea—the source of all the sighs, and of Nall. Following Mailin indoors, she said shyly, "I don't know anything about the sea."

"And now you have met it." Mailin laughed, nodding toward Nall.

Kat said stiffly, "I don't know anything about him, either."

"We meet each other first, and thus we learn."

Mailin seemed quite used to having a Rig asleep in her kitchen, stepping over him now and then as

88

she shifted the lids from pots and picked a knob of garlic from a wreath by the window.

Kat stood in the middle of the room with her hands behind her back. She cast shy, fierce looks at Nall, at his bare brown foot on the rumpled cotton. At last she said, "I don't know anything about the Rigi. They . . . we don't have any real ones, up there."

Mailin straightened from the pot; her eyes were last night's eyes. But all she said was, "Can you make tea?"

"Of course I can."

"Make tea, then, while I make soup."

So Kat padded self-consciously around the strange kitchen, hunting for kettle and mugs and looking timidly about her. The windowsills were full of herbs growing in cans and spoutless teapots. There were shelves full of burlap bags; a scarred table with an open book; cupboards full of bowls, mugs, and plates; pitchers with mended handles. The sieve was full of hickory nuts. There were flails and mattocks, saws and hammers, sickles and fishhooks and old coarse knives; there were round cheeses, a basket of onions, a fat red squash. The parrot mumbled half an apple and dropped the shreddings on the floor. Nothing in this room was polished or set straight, yet it had its own orderliness—that of use, or of the sea, which pushes things around not haphazardly but in answer to the moon.

The lizard was gone from the door frame. Kat looked cautiously for the bull snake, to be sure it was not in the same room she was, and found it still coiled neatly about its shovel at the farther hearth. When Kat raised her eyes from it she saw again the sealskin on the wall. It was very old, sewn with beads of silver, beads of jet—potent and terrible, with nothing looking out of its empty eyes.

Shivering, Kat came back to Nall and the fire. She said hesitantly, "My Auntie Jerash says the Rigi drown you."

"Did he drown you?"

"No . . ."

"Ah."

It was fish soup that Mailin was warming, adding bits of laver. When she had the new garlic in the pot, she shifted Nall casually from the hearth by pulling him, pallet and all; he did not stir.

"They sleep very deeply," she said. "They dream. More in winter, when it is cold; they huddle like seals, with the children in the middle."

"He *is* a seal, then," said Kat, very low.

"No." Mailin hung the pot from the chimney hook. "He is a man. We say 'The Rigi are seals' because the seal is their totem. One of my ancestors was a Rig."

"He *was*?"

"You see his sealskin. At least they say that was his skin. It was very long ago. He came of his own will—they did, in those days—so he kept his skin."

Kat grew very busy with the teapot. After a moment she asked carefully, "Your ancestor. Was . . . did he marry another Rig?"

"A Downshore girl. So because of them I sing the Rigi's song, and I dance the Seal on Long Night."

"The Rigi's song!" Boiling water slopped and hissed into the ashes. Kat said recklessly, "I sang that. I sang it over and over, and then he came."

"Ah!" said Mailin with delight. "So that is how you called. How did you come to know the Rigi's song?"

"There was an old woman in the market, long ago. She was little and fat and she kept the herb stall. She gave me an apple. I heard that song then. That's how I know your name, from her: 'Mailin is the best,' she said."

"That will have been Bikis."

"Where is she now?"

"She is dead. Who sang the song?"

"I never saw."

"One of us, the Rigi kin, of course."

"I saw nobody." Guiltily Kat cried, "If I called him . . . then is it my fault they tied him and took his skin, and made him swim?"

"No," said Mailin slowly. "I think Nall also was calling you."

As though he had heard his name, Nall spoke a foreign word clearly in his sleep, and uncurled his fist.

Mailin laughed. "He said, 'Soup'!"

"I never heard anybody call. I never."

Mailin ladled soup into two chipped green bowls and sat down cross-legged upon the hearth. "And they did not make him swim. They took his sealskin

91

and his name, and they cut off his long braid. They pulled the earrings from his ears—you will find the scars—and bound him, and took him to the Place of Bones, where they leave their dead. I know this because I know the stories. But they only left him there. It was he who chose to swim."

Kat cried in horror, "Why would they do that?"

"To cast him out. He might tell you why."

"I hate them!" Leaping to Nall, she laid both hands on his back. "I'll kill them!"

"In their way they are wise to take everything," said Mailin. "He chose to cross, and if you must swim those waters, it is best to swim them as naked as you can." She held out the green bowl. "Eat."

Kat cried, "I don't understand anything anymore!"

"I do not understand anything either." Mailin was cheerful. "Yet soup feeds me. Like these foolish kittens: They know nothing but supper, yet they will grow perfectly into cats."

She laughed and fell to. Because she was famished, Kat followed, settling herself cautiously next to Nall. Beck washed her kittens sternly with wet slaps of her tongue, and when Mailin set her empty bowl down on the hearth, Beck rose and washed that equally. Mailin stroked her.

"If you go west over the ocean toward the end of the world," said Mailin quietly, "you will come to a stony island called the Place of Bones. If you go west farther still you will come to other islands, low and green in the gray trough of the deep. That is where the Rigi live. And the end of the world will still be west over the ocean."

92

Kat put down her bowl for Beck. Surreptitiously she slid her hand under the blanket to touch Nall's back, warm as a peat fire; he came from just before the end of the world.

"I have not gone west over the ocean," said Mailin. In her voice there was a little longing. "But I know the Rigi's tales as I know their tongue. Those islands have few trees and much rock, heather and gorse and grass. There are no cattle, but the Rigi keep goats, little brown ones. The children tend them. In the summer the Rigi are brown like their goats, from the sun. But in winter they are pale, for they sleep and sleep in their low stone houses, rolled together like the seals. They will not kill seals except for the skins, one skin for every child that is born. That is the child's seal. Nall had a skin."

"They took it."

"They took his seal. That was the same as killing him, to them."

"He said that." Her hand lay secretly on his warm back. Defiantly she asked, "Then he is a bad man?"

"What is bad? What is good?"

Kat scowled, puzzled. It was common knowledge what was bad and what was good; or it had been.

"They are an unchanging people, the Rigi. That is almost who they are, for us: the changeless keepers, of the deep and of all that lies before the end of the world. Some people say the sun rises because of them, and the tide brings the fish. Our first songs came from them, we say, and the Plain tongue rose from their speech. From them we learned to build the Year Fire, to dance the Long Night, the Snake. . . . Oh, Lali, when we lost them we lost much. They are the source. But they are not . . . tolerant. Of change least of all. And this one— look at him!" She laughed, brushing the hair from Nall's determined face. "This one is change itself!"

"Even his name," said Kat. He had defied his tribe and slipped from death; he had crossed the water. And he had come to her. To her. In that instant she gave her whole heart to him in a torrent that left her hollow, as though it poured out of her through her warm hand. Yet her hand was secret and still.

The cheerful singing began again:

Out of the sea's grip, hup!
Out of those dark arms, hey!

This time Kat knew Pao's voice, and to hide her own feelings she asked Mailin boldly, "Is your husband Rigi kin, too?"

"Pao? No. Pao is of the Badger Clan. He is not my husband—we are not married. He is my man."

"Oh!" Kat did not know where to look. Auntie Jerash had been very clear about women who were not married. Kat withdrew her hand hastily from Nall's back and clasped it with the other.

"When I was young I was a wife," said Mailin gravely. "Now I am a woman."

To fill the lengthening silence Kat said desperately, "My mother was a wife. At least that part was all right, and nobody . . ." She stopped, the dull blood rising to her face.

"Lali," said Mailin. "Who was your mother, besides a wife?"

"She was a Hill woman." Shame made her surly.

"I thought so! I know that bright hair."

Kat put up one hand as though to hide behind it and said sullenly, "She died."

Mailin was unperturbed. "There are fine songs about that hair. It is the light on the mountains when the sun sets, or fire in the oak, or a crown. Did she sing those songs?"

"Not those." Kat twisted her hands miserably in her lap, adding suddenly, "I don't know her name even. All they ever called her was 'Ab Drem's wife.' "

"You never asked?"

"No." Kat thought of the sidelong looks, the whispers.

Out of the silence that followed, Mailin spoke as though to herself. "Hill women come to dance the Long Night. One could ask about her there."

"Father would never . . ." Kat was saying desperately to her hands, when to her relief footsteps rang on the stairs, and Pao entered whistling, the otter at his neck. Dai followed him, pink with happiness. He had a pipkin covered with greased paper in one hand and he was saying vigorously, "The bear is fattest right before the winter. . . ."

"I am fattest right before the winter myself," said Pao.

Dai gave him the pipkin and bobbed his head toward Mailin with a naked, hopeful look. To Kat he said, "All's well, sister."

"He's not back?"

Relief made him garrulous. "Not even waked. I took the mule to Graystone, easy as that." He surveyed her kindly. "Still, best get home."

Kat looked at Nall, plunged in sleep, and turned to Mailin a face of dismay.

Mailin said, "You will come again."

"Yes, I will." Kat hesitated, then laid her hand openly on Nall's back.

Pao gazed at her thoughtfully and stroked his beard. "Mailin," he said, "you and I should go down to the cow for just a moment, so that Dai can teach us about bear's fat. But someone must stay with this man."

"I will," Kat said instantly.

"Excellent," said Pao.

When the voices came muffled from under the verandah, she edged her knee up snugly against Nall, laying her cheek down on the scratchy blanket. Pushing back his hair she found the half-healed scar where his earring had been tugged away; she put her hand over just the lobe so that she would not see it.

"My name is Katyesha Marashya n'Ab Drem," she whispered. "Is it true you called me?"

His eyebrows twitched, but he slept as sound as ever.

"Nall!"

"Soup," he said distinctly in that other tongue, and smiled in his sleep.

12

"KATYESHA MARASHYA," said Ab Drem to no one;
no one was there except the black mule, between
whose ears he gazed at the homeward track. "Katyesha for obedience, Marashya for prudence . . ."

He held her name as he would warm a coin
between his fingers, and gave the mule a perfunctory
whack on the head with his riding stick. "And n'Ab
Drem for me. I named her well. With luck she'll
have a new master now, and a new name. A good
name! Katyesha Marashya n'Ab . . . n'Ab . . ."

But for his life he could not remember the name

of Ab Harlan's youngest son, though he had spoken to Harlan just that morning.

He had risen late from the cedar bed, refreshed, though as always obscurely uneasy and a little groggy with sedative and rum. After a brushing and a setting right from his brother's wife, he had gone directly to Ab Harlan; they had talked of the brandy cellaring, and after a while they had talked of the other matter. "Eh!" Harlan had said. "Sixteen? And your own assets?" His sons were at work behind him at the books, but they all looked alike: biggish, fairish. Harlan had jerked his head toward the youngest. But was it Nate, or Shay, or Desso, or Barim?

"That's soon known," Ab Drem said aloud, for Harlan and his youngest son were coming to Cliff Tooth House tomorrow evening for a game of War.

With another whack Ab Drem turned the mule through the gate, into the teeth of the wind. The mule, as was its habit, made directly for the byre and had to be driven away from it toward the house with curses and blows. Dai rose from his slouch on the bench by the byre door and louted across the yard to take the reins.

"Eh," said Ab Drem. He slid down stiffly and took the saddlebags. With his hand on the latch he turned back and said shortly, "Yesterday. You dealt with that?"

"Took him Downshore. Sir."

"Eh."

Ab Drem entered Cliff Tooth House and shut the door against the wind.

98

This was his, the orderly territory which he had forced the world to yield him. The girl was there, of course; it could not be so orderly without her. Jerash was right—what would he do for a housekeeper when Katyesha was married?

She stood at the white hearth, holding her bony old cat.

"Eh," he said to her, and since he had spent the morning dealing with the matter, he looked at her almost tenderly. A good girl, to make a good wife. What a foolish duckling of a baby she had been! An undecorous child with her petticoats yanked sideways, never with both shoes.

"You've shaped well," he told her, and she stared at him. The old cat, which did not like being held like a baby with its feet up, snarled in a singsong, and switched its tail. "Wash your hands. I'll have my tea."

Without a word she went to wash, fetched the kettle, and filled it at the water bucket. It seemed to him that she watched him covertly, with bewilderment or trouble. He felt annoyed with Dai; she must look good for Harlan.

"Still upset by yesterday, are you?"

Hooking the kettle onto the chain, she stopped. A terrible dull blush rose over her neck, her arms; but she shook her head, and settled the handle with a click.

Ab Drem jingled in his pockets and held out a worn brass coin. "Here," he said. "Buy yourself some little pretty thing."

She took the coin slowly, without speaking.

He was not usually uneasy with silence, but something prodded him to fill it. "Eh! And how's your old cat?"

Her face waked a little, and at last she spoke. "I met some people. They have kittens. Six."

"You want a kitten! Surely. Get yourself a kitten, eh!" He eased himself into the stiff-backed chair by the fire. "Of course, get rid of the old one first."

She cast him an unbelieving stare but he was tugging at his boots, summoning her to help him.

"Tomorrow night we have important guests. This house must be clean from top to bottom, cleaner than your aunt could make it. I must have bread, and ham, and brandy, and a roast. And you in your best, girlie; I won't have Ab Harlan think you're a tinker's daughter."

He thought she would say, "Ab Harlan?" but she said, "Tomorrow?" in a voice of dismay. "I was to go to market."

"Dairois will go. You are outdoors too much. You are getting brown, child; what husband wants a wife the color of a saddle?"

"Husband," she said slowly, standing with the lid of the kettle in her hand.

"My tea." He was irked with talk, and put his feet up. She brought it, with a new biscuit in the saucer. "I trust you have polished the board for War."

"No." She said suddenly, "Yesterday I did a wicked thing."

"Eh?" He stared at her, astonished, over the rising steam.

"I kicked the polishing rag into the fire."

Obedience, prudence. Why, the honest child!
"Remorse is laudable." Contentedly, he took the
cup from her hand. "You must pray more, and never
kick the latch."

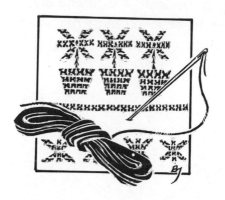

13

Bring water from the cistern with the yoke.
Milk the cow.

Clean the hearth, clean the floor.

Set straight the stool, the stiff table, the stiff chairs that were already straight.

Dust everything.

Polish.

The wind blew. Kat had a new polishing rag that she had torn from her old skirt, for scrub as she might the bloodstains would not vanish from it— Nall's blood. As she polished she sang the Rigi's song under her breath, fiercely and secretly and fast.

She sang only when Ab Drem was not there. He was in and out, back and forth to Graystone House, fussing like a hen. When he was in he kept his eye on her: finding dust on the wood box, despising the size of the roast, fretting whether the bread would rise. When she could she avoided him, but he so nagged her that she decided he must be entering that mysterious affliction of the aged at which Auntie Jerash had vaguely hinted, menopause.

"Sit and rest, Father," she said. "I'll get your pipe."

"Eh!" he scowled, rooting among his books. "Wipe that smudge from your forehead!"

So with bucket and cloth and broom she passed the day, pausing to baste the roast and to beat down the brown bread dough with her fists. Because Ab Drem knew nothing about Nall she felt secretive, exalted. She helped her father off with his boots, on with his jacket, off with his greatcoat, on with his vest. Yet it was not Cliff Tooth House where she worked.

Nall, Nall . . . She tried his name with hers— Katyesha Marashya n'Ab Nall. It was not her father's hearth she scrubbed, but Nall's. She straightened Nall's table, polished Nall's mantel and Nall's plates. She baked for him, four loaves instead of two. The hand outstretched demanding tea was a brown hand; she brought Nall driftwood for his fire.

"I want that game board shining," said Ab Drem.

"Yes, sir."

Dreaming, she brought Nall milk and water with the yoke. He laid his brown hand on her waist; with his eyes as gray as rain he said, "It is time you were married. You knew I needed you, and you came when I called."

"You knew I needed a patch on my good trousers," said Ab Drem. "Two weeks ago I told you."

"I'll mend them now, sir," said Kat.

And then dinner was done. Because her legs were short, Kat sat with her feet propped primly on a footstool, her very polished slippers just peeping from under the hem of her gray silk skirt. Heavy and cool, the skirt had rustled about her thighs as she served supper, making her feel mysterious and important and subdued. The men, or men and boy, had pushed back their chairs and smoked.

The boy hadn't smoked before and it made him sick. Kat felt pity for him. He was younger than she was, pale pink and blond, and when he was old he would look exactly like Ab Harlan. The worst was that his name was Queelic.

Unless spoken to, women did not speak, but she had offered Queelic plums in brandy with compassion. He had blushed and turned his face away. Why, Kat thought kindly, he's as great a dolt as Dai.

Ab Harlan she did not like. He was fat and white, and as she served and cleared his little pig eyes had followed her with a sticky lasciviousness. The talk at the table had been dull, in monosyllables and all business, price, and weight. Kat had not cared; with her thoughts elsewhere she had cleared the table and brought the board for War. Dai, muttering excuses, had fled; all Upslope knew that Dai could not play War.

Women, of course, did not play. As the evening lengthened, Kat, her slippers prim on the footstool, held her elbows in and labored over the embroidery in her lap. Among the gruff cries of "Kill!" she thought of Nall, but here he seemed endangered and she put the image of him away in safety and secret. Instead she watched the game—the baron's straight pounce, the multiple little steps of the slaves. She had wondered before why among the pieces for War there were no animals. Perhaps, she thought, you can't teach a seal to kill somebody.

There were no animals in her embroidery, either. There were tiny stiff flowers in pots, and flowers in vases, and garlands, and bouquets. There was even a tiny sheaf of wheat—that was her favorite—but there was no mouse to peer from behind it, not even a dove to settle among the neat rosettes.

Kat liked to sew—it was part of life, what you had to do to have clothes—but what she liked was to take a piece of flat cloth, mark it and cut it and stitch it and lo! it became a pair of trousers, or a shirt with tucks at the collar, or a skirt. But Auntie Jerash had been scandalized. "Will you be married plain as a fishwife? Embroidered shifts and petticoats, with sheets to match, young lady." Once a month, so that Kat would not be slack, she reviewed the growing pile of dull goods in the old dowry chest that had come from the hills with Kat's mother.

From where she sat Kat could see the chest full on, with its bright copper hinges and brass lock. Inside, the dutiful pile of linens crowded the slight bundle that was the skirt and blouse her mother had worn when she came from the hills with Ab Drem.

Now that was embroidery! Sometimes when Ab Drem was away Kat unfolded it to look. There were snakes and bears and foxes and deer and even a marmot, all in red on the white and blue wool. There were birds—hawks and eagles, ducks and cranes, chickadees, a tomtit. There were flowers, too, but none in pots. All were growing out of the embroidered ground, mixed in with wheat stalks, oats or barley, and with trees. Kat remembered being very small, stroking a red bear with one finger.

If I could do what I wanted, she thought, I'd embroider birds. And otters, and a tortoise, and a lizard. Also a seal.

She straightened her back and looked at Queelic, who was not doing what he wanted, either. Being the junior, he had to be spy and he was just as bad at it as Dai. He looked so miserable that she smiled at him. He scowled and ducked his head.

Suddenly Ab Harlan was saying, "Eh, enough." Though the game was not over he pushed back his chair, picked his ear, and looked about him for his walking stick. Ab Drem was clearly dismayed but Ab Harlan said, "It grows late. The evening was not for the game, Drem." Polishing the gold knob of his cane with the palm of one fat hand, he looked at Kat as though it were she whom he stroked. She looked away. "I'll sleep on it. Come to me tomorrow. But not till after lunch."

As she held his greatcoat for him, Kat wondered whether the business of the evening had been cinnamon, or brandy, or gold; they had hardly spoken a phrase without a number in it.

"Good evening, Drem."

Queelic stumbled over the tall threshold on his way out.

"Stop it!" cried Ab Drem. "I don't understand you!"

For they beseeched, they called; but they were animals and he could not reason with them. They were gray-eyed, wet-furred, and no word could he fathom from their importuning until at last he heard, "Father! Father!" and looked down, where a little one of them was clinging to his knee. He snatched it up, shook it. "Stop it!" he shouted. But still it wailed, "Father!"

He woke in the dark with a sob. The world was shaking; but it was only Katyesha, hammering on the doors of his box bed. "Father! Father!"

"Stop it," he said, and unlatched the doors. They swung open to her standing drowned in her great white nightgown, all eyes. She carried a candle.

"Are you all right?" she cried.

"I dreamed," he said, wiping his face with his hand. "Be damned, I dreamed, I dreamed!"

In the chimney the wind boomed like a drum; so very long was this night till morning, almost the longest night. She shut her mouth and looked at him with that look she had—so like her mother, a ghost. To make her turn away he said, "Woman, I will have tea," and swung his thin old legs in their nightshirt over the edge of the bed.

Turn she did, and moved about the hearth, but all the time she glanced at him over her shoulder.

"I must get a cedar bed," he said. "I must speak to the doctor."

He watched her wake the cold hearth and set the kettle. That worthless boy was not even home, no doubt out in the byre like an animal; but here was the child tending her father in the middle of the night, her bare feet cold on the stones.

"You're a good girl," he told her suddenly. He was so soon to lose her. "Take tea with me."

She threw him a look that was half alarm and half some other thing. Grief? Scorn? But when she had settled him in his stiff chair she fetched another chair from the table and sat on the edge of it with her feet hooked over the rung.

Ab Drem had nothing else to say; he did not talk to women. Together they waited for the kettle to boil. Behind her on her mother's old dowry chest he saw, spread out, those white and blue embroidered clothes. She saw him looking and hastily forstalled him.

"I'm learning a new stitch. I fetched them out to see."

"Do what you will," he said roughly.

The kettle boiled. She poured water into the clean white pot, filling the air with the honey smell of camomile, and sat down again on the edge of the chair. Quite suddenly she asked, "Father, how did you and my mother come to meet?"

Panic rose in him. He had not allowed himself to set words, or even thoughts, to that in years; when the question came from this bit of the woman's flesh and his own, he had no answer.

Having no answer made him angry. "Shameless!" he snapped.

But she sat looking at him, so like the girl, the girl: brown neck, white breast. Red hair. As though it were pressed out of him he said, "I don't remember."

But he did remember: the red sun on the slope, her hair ablaze with it. Her brown hands.

"Father . . ."

"Stop it!" he cried. He must stop it. "Beauty is nothing," he said harshly, like a cry. "It rots, it dies."

She was silent.

He wiped his face. As though from the air around him he gathered his authority and shouldered it like armor.

"Shameless!" he said. "What will your husband think of you, when you are married?"

"Husband," she echoed, and it seemed to him that she had spoken so before.

"If anyone will have you, which remains to be seen."

That silenced her. He remembered that tomorrow he would speak to Ab Harlan, and was comforted; he emptied his cup noisily and stood.

"There is no vice in a woman like a loose tongue," he said. "See that you deserve what will befall you."

She said nothing, nor looked at him; she twisted her fingers together in her lap. He looked down on her tangled red hair.

"Cover your head," he said. "Go to bed. Put those rags back in the chest; I cannot bear to look at them."

Seated on his mattress, swinging his legs back into the dark bed, he paused; he looked around the doors. She still sat by the hearth with her feet curled up, her head bowed.

"Daughter," he said, "thank you for the tea."

14

THE SHORTEST DAY rose late out of mist and smoke.

Coming back from milking in the gray light, Kat saw distant Scythe Road outlined in travelers' fires. The air was cold and laced with the smell of many burnings.

At the hearth, Ab Drem, with one boot on, was eating the porridge she had made for him. Usually so silent, this morning he was full of comment and distraction: "It's early yet," and "Busy day, busy day." His face was haggard, eager. He said nothing of the night before.

She left him alone. Fussy, harrying, he called her over to help him with his boots, his waistcoat, his hat. She obeyed him hastily; she wished him in the sea, on the moon—anywhere away from the house. Long before noon he had her fetch out the mule, and shouting back over his shoulder with vexation and admonishment he rode off into the mist which scudded over the rocks.

Snatching up her laden market basket, she latched the door behind her and ran Downshore.

For fear of the strangers on Scythe Road, she took the cattle path, turning at the travelers' rest down the alley to the market. The town was full of foreigners with strange clothes, strange speech. At a distance she saw the Hill women in groups, laughing with their children; they always came to Long Night without their men. Kat hesitated, stared. But when a woman turned toward her, smiling, she scuttled on with one hand to her kerchief. No one was from Upslope, and no one paid her any heed. She ran to the fish stalls, calling "Suni!" over the mackerel heads.

Suni came cheerfully into the sunlight, lifting her daughter onto her hip.

"Lali Kat!"

"How do you do," said Kat, suddenly shy.

"So many people, aren't there! The whole world comes to Long Night. Even Upslope, the men anyway—they don't dance, though, they just drink and watch the women. Your brother was here, with Pao. They're making fish glue."

"*Fish* glue," Kat said blankly. There was no room in her for any thought but Nall.

"The brewer's ox has a split hoof. They were going to soak linen in fish glue and bind it up, they said." She laughed. "They *stank!*"

"I made bread." Kat offered a long loaf, asking very carefully, "Did Pao . . . He didn't say anything?"

"About your Rig?"

"My Rig!" Instantly she was drowned in a blush, even her hands on the basket handle. But Suni did not laugh. In a burst of confidence Kat added, "His name is Nall."

"They were being like men—very busy with their fish glue, and nothing important was important. But Pao said, 'Well, it's luck or storms!' He meant your Rig will live."

"He'll live. . . ."

"So the luck is yours, or the storms, whichever." She spoke gravely over Rosie's fair head. "Very great luck, Lali. A Rig! He can't dance the Long Night yet, but we'll dance it for him. Will you dance tonight?"

"I'm on my way to Pao's house," said Kat evasively.

"To see your Rig. Here—take this mackerel to Mailin. She'll make soup."

"I've brought soup. Nall likes it." Kat put the fish in her basket, this time careful to say "Thank you!" as she turned toward the throng. She turned back. "Suni. Is your man . . . Is he your husband?"

"Rosie married us," said Suni, swinging the baby on her hip. "Didn't you then!"

"But is he your husband?"

"He's my man. He's with us." She broke a crust from the bread and Rosie took it in her fist. "That's all there ever is. She's got another tooth, look."

Kat put her finger in the reluctant pink mouth.

"Don't go by the beach," said Suni. "They're building the Year Fire and you'll never get through. Go left past the portals and down the path."

Looking back, Kat saw Rosie flapping her fat hand aimlessly in a wave, Suni laughing.

The broad alley was full of young stevedores with bare backs and short trousers, bundles of driftwood for the Year Fire on their shoulders. Shouting townsfolk were shifting a decayed harrow and a shattered bedstead in the same direction, as well as the downed boughs of cherry trees, turnip crates, a tabletop split beyond repair—all to pile upon the Year Fire stack. When she came out of town among the middens Kat could see it, large as a house, and hear the murmur of the crowd that swarmed around it like ants on a hot afternoon. The sound was as awesome as the sea.

She trudged in sand.

The nearer she drew to the house with its fluttering flags the higher rose in her a strange anxiety, and the slower she walked, until she stopped altogether.

"I'm only *visiting* him," she said angrily to no one. Even Auntie Jerash made charity visits. "Somebody had to bring the bread." And she strode forward, her heart sinking and her shoulders very straight.

Suni was right: It stank unbelievably of fish, whatever they were doing under the verandah. Kat stood irresolute in the shadow of the steps until Dai looked up, his mouth full of linen strips.

He and Pao had built a little fire in the open, and on it a pot bubbled. The black cow with the cracked udder was tethered to the pilings, lowing resonantly now and then.

"Lali Kat!" smiled Pao, raising one hand. He looked broad and calm as a mountain, his unbending leg propped out in front of him. The lizard clung to his shirt front.

She curtsied stiffly. Dai smiled at her around the linen strips; she was not used to Dai's smile.

Pao pointed upward with his thumb. "Someone waits for you upstairs," he said.

She wished to her boot soles that she had not come. Holding up the basket, she said loudly, "Mailin. I brought Mailin some things."

"Ah!" The thumb remained aloft. "Mailin is upstairs too. And the otter. They couldn't stand the smell of us."

She would give the bread to Pao, and flee; Dai could bring back the basket. But Dai was ignoring her. He spat out the linen, and whistled. She turned from him in reckless despair and rattled up the steps.

Nall was sitting against the front door in the sunshine.

He had balanced an enormous bowl of soup on his upraised knee, and now ate as he had slept: fiercely. He wore borrowed trousers, and his bandaged leg stuck straight out in front of him, like Pao's. At her step he raised his face slowly, like an animal from its meat.

"You," he said.

Pao had shaved him and cut his hair. His eyes were the same, as gray as ocean; but the rest of his face was a stranger's. Vivid and male, it shone newshaven as her father's on a meeting-day morning. All the crescent-shaped muscles around his mouth were startlingly plain and smooth.

She was undone.

Clinging to the basket, she stammered righteously, like Auntie Jerash, "Did . . . I hope . . . Did you sleep well?"

He did not drop his eyes; they were tired and clear.

She thrust out the basket as though to fend him off with it. "I brought bread. And things. Soup."

He did not move to take it. "Kat."

"Katyesha Marashya n'Ab Drem!" she gasped. "Where's Mailin?"

But as in the byre he said, dismayed, "You had red hair!"

Her hand flashed to her head; all was secure. Yet she loosened the knot and pulled away the kerchief.

"Yes!" He raised his good hand toward her.

She stepped backward in a panic, almost tumbling down the steps. But he did not have the strength to rise and touch her, and that made him a little safe;

116

as on the beach she hunkered down beyond arm's reach.

They stared at each other. Under their feet the cow mooed. Nall said thoughtfully, "That animal shouts too much. It shouts all the time."

"That's a cow."

"A cow."

They were silent. The cow shouted. At last Kat said with stern reprimand, like her aunt, "You're letting that soup get cold."

But to her dismay he shuffled himself to one side, making room for her to put her back against the door; the same impulse that had made her pull the kerchief from her head made her sit down next to his shoulder, not touching him. To cover her confusion she asked him severely, "Would you care for bread?" and took the last loaf from the basket; then her resolution deserted her and she added shyly, "I made it for you."

"For me!" He held the brown loaf in his brown hand.

"I'll break it," she said hastily. Balancing the bowl on her lap, she made him keep the spoon and gave him the best piece, the end one. "It has poppy seeds."

They ate in silence. Out of the side of her eye she watched the lively sinew of his forearm, his short thigh, his shaven cheek; he watched her warmly and openly, chewing. The weals on his bare ankle itched, and he scratched them. The sunny wood of the door smelled almost hot; every now and then a whiff of fish glue rose through the cracks in the verandah and they both stopped eating until it passed.

"Smells very strange," he said at last.

"This side of the water!"

The words spoke themselves; her hand flew to her mouth. For the first time in her life she had made a joke.

He stared; then he laughed with his whole body, as a puppy barks.

Blind with giggles, Kat still managed to keep the bowl upright. Something gripped her knee; looking down, she saw Nall's brown hand.

He said passionately, "This is a good place where you have brought me. I will thank you for the rest of my life."

"Nall, oh, Nall!" said Kat, just as Mailin, going out for water with the otter on her shoulder, opened the door behind them; together they toppled backward into the house, along with the soup.

15

"TELL ME WHY they killed you."

Kat sat on the edge of the verandah, vigorously swinging her feet. She wore an old shirt and culottes of Mailin's; her own, the soup scrubbed out of them, were drying by the fire. "Why did they kill you?" she said again.

Nall sat with his back to the balustrade. She could scarcely bear to look at him, at his brown throat rising up over his collarbone; she looked across the curved bay instead, to the rising stack of the Year Fire, unlit till night.

"Your hair is the color of the sun," he said softly,

as though that answered her. "At morning, at night—the two edges of the world." He put up his hand absently to touch her curls; she crouched like something young that will be eaten if it stirs.

"Where you come from, is the sun the same?" She asked him just to hear his voice. She had never heard anyone speak like that: easily, unembarrassed.

"The same. In winter I dreamed the sun—that I called it down, it carried me. When they left me at the Place of Bones I dreamed again—that it burned away the ropes and took me up." Rueful humor creased his face. "That was a dream! So I broke the ropes myself, and I swam."

"Why did they leave you there?" He did not call her "girlie"; she would ask him every question in the world.

"Because I sang."

"You *sang*?"

He was almost shy. "I sang new songs. They come to me—they want to be sung. The elders never like new songs. . . . My father is an elder."

"My father wants to be a deacon."

"What is a deacon?"

"They wear a special hat."

With his knuckles, he stroked her wrist. He made sure of the world with his body, like Small Gray. She sat very still and said carefully, "You made up a new song?"

"I profaned an old one." He was grinning, but grave. "You sang it."

"The Rigi's song!"

120

"The Old Song. It is the oldest in . . . in this crossing tongue."

"The Plain tongue."

"Yes. For the Old Song I . . . found new words. But I was trouble for the elders before that. I was born trouble."

"I was born trouble, too," she said loyally, and the thought comforted her.

"Yes? I was to be a priest. But that is bondage! The songs are guarded, always the same." He made a forceful gesture with one hand, from his belly to his throat. "New songs rise. I shape them. But this time . . ."

"I *knew* you weren't bad!" she interrupted him with fervent sympathy. "I knew it. What stupid people, to punish you for a song!"

"Where you come from," he said wistfully, "you can sing whatever comes to you?"

"Oh . . ." She swung her feet hard. "Tell me . . . keep telling that story."

He laid his palm casually on hers. "At times of crossing," he said, "we sing the Old Song. This time we sang for a woman giving birth. Her pain was too long. . . . Nothing happened. . . . I rose, I sang the new words that came to me. The babies came, twins."

"So that was a good thing!"

"The babies were half seal. No arms: short like this, a seal's arms."

Your mother bore a demon child.

"Such children belong to Mother Death. We must

121

give them back to her. The elders said they must give me back, too. I profaned the song."

From under the hand of her horror Kat whispered, "It was the song that did it?"

"No." His voice was serene. "Those children were seals in their mother's belly long before I sang. They chose it."

"My brother was born with a bear's face." It was the first she had ever told anyone.

"What is a bear?"

"Oh . . . *Ouma. Katim na*. They live in the hills. They are big, big like Pao: furry all over, brown and red. Teeth. Claws." She reared up her hands like forepaws, to show him.

He was puzzled. "He is very hairy, your brother, but if I do not shave I am the same."

"No, no. Another brother. He died."

"Yes? But those seal babies did not die right away. They waved their little arms and cried to go to the Mother. So the elders killed me, there in front of the tribe. Then they took me with the babies in a boat, to the Place of Bones—that is the Mother's place—and they tied me among the skulls of the ancestors that are all picked clean by crabs. They did not have to tie the babies. Then they sailed back to the Home Stone."

"They *left* the *babies*?"

"They gave them back. Nights are cold now. They died very soon."

"You saw it!"

"I was two days breaking the ropes. It rained, and that was water. No food. There were crabs, but . . ."

He hesitated. "The crabs ate the babies. I could not eat the crabs."

"Oh!" she cried. "Those are horrible people! They should be killed!"

He said softly, "I am one of them."

"They cast you out!"

"I am still . . . who I am," he said doggedly. "Like those babies. I came from my father and my mother."

In despair she turned her face away.

He said quietly, "My mother watched them kill me. I saw her at the crowd's edge. She did not cry. My father pulled the earrings from my ears. I thought, They are monsters, and I came from them. I am a monster."

He put his hand to her cheek and she looked up, flinching. "But I swam. It does not matter. Good, bad—it has washed away. They are still there, in their own life—and I am here." He laid his hand on his own chest. "I am! Nall."

She echoed him: "Long Wave."

"Katyesha Marashya n'Ab Drem . . . that means red?"

"It means stupid," she said violently. "It's all my father's."

"A new name will come."

"No." She could not stop shivering. "That's all I've got."

From under the verandah rose first the cow's voice and then Dai's; he was singing the lullaby in the Hill tongue, but he had embellished it cheerfully until it sounded like Pao's.

Kitam na, hup!
Kitam yao, hey!

"You sang that song before," said Nall, listening. "That is a different tongue."

"It's the Hill tongue," she told him listlessly. "That song is about bears."

"You are a Hill woman?"

"I'm not!" But she did not want to be her father's daughter either. "My mother was a Hill woman. That's why my hair is red. Don't stare at me!" Crossly she reared up her hands again, to hide her face. "It's red. I was born like that."

He said gravely, "You are a bear, a red one."

"Then you're a seal, so there!" She thought he was mocking her about her brother.

"I was." His voice was full of grief. "Now I am a man."

He turned to look out across the water. They could see the whole of the beach, a sickle of white sand to the docks. People were busy on it like ants—dashing, gesticulating, carrying tiny bundles.

"And those are ants." She was afraid she had hurt him, anxious to make peace. "That's their anthill."

"That is a house they build, the house of the year."

"I thought it was a fire."

"Your people build no Year Fire?"

"My people don't do anything. Much. The women polish things, and the men play War."

"Polish? . . ."

"Tell me all about Year Fires," she said quickly.

He gave her a warm look. "We bring driftwood. We pile it up. Best if it was a made thing that came to us floating. And anything broken, old—the heather tedding from the sleep place, full of fleas—out! Onto the fire stack. On Long Night we light it, and all the animals dance."

"The animals dance!"

"You, me—we dance for them. You will dance for that red bear. I know."

"What will you dance for?"

"I am lame. I will not dance." But then he put his head back with a grimace. "The seal! There will be other years, other fires. Until I die, I will dance the seal."

She cast about for something to comfort him. "It doesn't matter if you can't dance. You can swim. Seals swim." She swung her legs again, her white human feet. "I can't swim."

"You cannot *swim*?"

"It's all air up there where I come from. Rocks, ashes, wind. No water."

"Where I come from," he said slowly, "all is water, water. The moon is very close. All together we swim, we sing." He laid his hand earnestly on her thigh. "I will teach you to swim."

"In the sea?" Fear stroked her. "It's very big."

"You swim in only a little bit at a time." He flashed his tired grin.

"Maybe . . ."

"When you are ready I will teach you."

They watched the distant humans bringing bales and bundles, casting them down. She thought of putting her own hand over his, on her thigh; she could not.

He said, "You will dance tonight?"

Because she was ashamed of everything, of all her fears, she said recklessly, "I might. I might go ask the Hill women about my mother." When she had said it she was horrified, and shut her mouth.

He said only, "Dance, Kat."

It was her name, from his mouth; she remembered that night before the hearth, his breath in the hollow of her neck. "I can't . . . I can't swim," she gasped. "I mean I can't dance, either. I never learned."

"To dance, to swim . . ." His voice was harsh with weariness. "To sing. To dream. They are the same." He put his head down on his knee. "They are all to stay alive."

She did not understand anything but his exhaustion, and said timidly, "You should go back to sleep."

"I should dream," he agreed, or corrected her. "Tonight they sing the Old . . . the Rigi's song." He turned and touched her face. "You called me."

"I didn't know I was calling anybody!" she cried, almost a wail.

He said nothing; after a moment she asked haltingly, "Did you call *me*?"

"I do not know." He looked west over the empty water. "I do not know what I call to me when I sing."

16

THE BRIEF DAY was closing, turning toward the cold west as a seal turns to plunge from scarp to sea. On the old striped pallet Nall, sleeping, dove through immeasurable deeps of dream; at Cliff Tooth House the hearth was unswept, Ab Drem's supper not begun, and Moss most certainly lowing to be milked. Yet Kat lingered, dallying into her dry clothes that must have shrunk in the washing, for they felt irksome, tight, and small. Beck nursed her kittens. As the light paled Dai came hastily, smelling of fish glue, with rags and remedies in a hempen bag over his shoulder.

"We'll see to the oxen and the dancers. Me and
Pao." His eyes were dark, exultant as he turned
away. "I'm a healer—they say so." From the verandah steps he shouted back, "Milk the cow!" and
vanished into the rising night.

Milk the cow! Kat thought angrily, although he
had always ordered her to milk the cow. I'm not his
daughter! I'm not his slave!

Mailin also moved quietly about, settling the
parrot, stowing salves and linen into a carrying
cloth. "I too shall go," she said. "I am always needed
at the dance, and this Rig has his dreams to heal
him. You?"

"I'm going home," said Kat quickly, before Mailin
could say anything about the Hill women at the
dance, about her mother. She tied the strings of her
cloak; it was so heavy and so long. With her eyes
on Nall's shadowy mouth, she asked, "How did you
meet your hus—How did you meet Pao?"

"Pao's knee was smashed between his dory and a
fishing boat. I tried to mend it but I could not."

"And then you just came to live at his house?"

"This house is mine."

"*Your* house!"

"It was my mother's."

Kat was pulling on her boots; head bent, she said
savagely, "I can't go to Long Night. My father
would never let me."

"Ah."

"Anyway, if I went, how could I ask about my
mother? I don't even know her name."

"Ah."

Then, without looking up, Kat whispered, "I might slip out at midnight. I might. I could go up to those Hill women and say, 'Have you heard of a Hill woman who married an Upslope man?' "

"Your red hair is your welcome."

"My father says I am shameless."

"Are you?"

"No." She rose and took her basket. "I'm ashamed of everything, all the time."

Mailin had finished her preparation, leaving Nall a little fire and banking the rest against the distant morning. From the far cold hearth she lifted down the ancient sealskin and folded it over her arm; she shouldered the carrying cloth and doused the lamp.

It was time for supper and father and cow. With the stubbornness of the child who will have one more story, Kat said, "You never told me why the Rigi don't come back." She crouched to touch Nall's cheek. "It isn't fair that he has to be alone, and hasn't anybody."

Mailin turned from the dark door. With the sealskin in both hands, she came back to the hearth, spreading it in the dim light; Kat saw the dense silver furn worn off in patches, the bells, the faded red embroidery of whirlpools, ripples, waves.

"A sealskin brings a good price in the south," said Mailin, "since the traders came."

Kat did not answer. Mailin shook the skin and it chimed and glinted like water. "It was so long ago that now it is just a story; but time was when the Rigi crossed to us, they say, in their black hide boats. They danced the Long Night with us, and the Snake. Sometimes they stayed; we had children, and were lucky."

Her voice was tranquil, without anger. "Then Upslope came. They had fine goods, they had money; they hired us, the coastal hunters. For each baby born the Rigi killed one holy seal, but the hired hunters killed by the hundreds. They say that the Rigi cried, 'You murder the tribe!' and begged us to remember our ancestors. But we were deaf with the clink of coin, and what have the Rigi ever been to Upslope? Beasts, bad dreams."

Almost inaudibly Kat said, "My father is a trader."

Mailin shrugged. "My father was a hunter. And he was Rigi kin! We loved the Rigi but we sold them, for cinnamon and brandy and gold."

She smoothed the sealskin in her hands. "Then one Long Night, they say, a gang of Upslope youths killed a Rig. They clubbed him like a seal, and took his skin. And that was the end of it; they never came again."

Kat said, in a voice as soft as the embers' hiss, "They told me it was my mother who was bad." And in an outburst that made Nall flinch and stir, "It isn't *me* who ought to be ashamed!"

"Lali, if you have learned only that, then there has been much healing." Mailin sighed. "We still kill seals for hire. Yet we long for the Rigi as for the tide's returning; we call and call, singing that song you know, and now and then a Rig comes to us like a gift, like hope. He is the first in a long time." She stood in the dark, a tall shadow. "They say the Rigi

come to Upslope in nightmares. Maybe Upslope is
calling too, in its way."

She folded the sealskin over her arm, and its bells
chimed faintly. Nall in dream cried, "No!" and
Mailin stilled him with her hand on his heart.

"Go now," she said to Kat. "The dance begins."

17

"WAR IS MATHEMATICS," said Ab Drem. "The best discipline."

He said it aloud even though he was alone, as though he needed to hear it. He was playing War, left hand against right, and the left was winning. How his hands loved the gamesmen, their efficient shapes! He held the white chancellor, and because he was alone and happy he did what he had not done since he was a little boy: He pressed the hard, cool china to his cheek.

Ab Drem played War in a rage of joy.

He had come home before the dusk to find his

house empty and cold, the hearth unswept. Yet he had scarcely noticed it. He had tied the mule at the door, pulled off his boots with the jack, waked the fire himself, and fetched a toddy with no more thought than, Damn the boy! and Where's the child? The child!

He had so much to give her. He could not be angry but thought only, Good girl. Fetching the fish, the milk. Oh, my child! and set the game board for himself.

For she was his redemption.

He had stood tensely before Ab Harlan's bare accounts table while the man picked his teeth and dealt with sundry matters that his pale sons brought for him to correct, revise. At last Harlan said, "Eh. Drem," and, rising, led him into the inner office with the hearth, the two straight chairs. Once there he turned without preamble and said, "Eh. I'll use you. And the girl will do well."

"Sir!" Ab Drem said, faint with conquest.

"A little drink on it." Ab Harlan fetched down the decanter and two glasses. "So! In a month's time. Get them started at it. Eh?"

"Sir!" His hand shook as he held the glass.

Harlan had looked at him shrewdly with his small eyes. "Drem. The little matter of your wife. It is forgotten. We'll see you a deacon yet."

"Sir!" With dog's eyes of adoration, Ab Drem raised his glass and said, "To this union!"

"May they dream not!"

They had clinked their glasses, downed the brandy, and shaken hands; slapping Drem's back,

Ab Harlan propelled him out into the accounting room and returned abruptly to the son who stood patiently at his desk, one forefinger marking the sum of a column. Was it Queelic? Ab Drem had not been sure—they all looked so much alike—and he himself, reeling with brandy and triumph, could scarcely breathe.

"Next week to arrange matters," Ab Harlan said absently. "You, of course, join us tomorrow. It is the new year."

"Sir!"

Ab Drem had gone immediately to Graystone House, to Ab Jerash and Ab Seroy. They had not played War. They talked avidly, joyously; they plotted, called Ab Drem "Deacon," downed walnuts and brandy and fruit. Ab Jerash's wife watched enviously from the kitchen, slapping Missa's fingers from the figs; her two eldest daughters were given in contract for weddings in the summer—to good men, but not to Ab Harlan's son.

As dusk fell, Ab Drem had risen and said, "I'll be gone. I'll tell the girl."

Ab Seroy said lazily, "Tell her she can't have a latch on the inside of her box bed anymore," and Ab Jerash said, "Tell her she's a good child."

His wife spoke suddenly from the kitchen: "She will sleep in silk."

"She won't sleep." Ab Seroy broke a fig with his thumb. "Not for a while."

Ab Drem had left them. He rode the mule into the teeth of the wind and was glad of it, for the violent air matched his joy. He almost wanted to sing; but the thought frightened him, and he thrashed the mule instead. He tied it clumsily at the door of Cliff Tooth House and made himself comfortable. The discipline of War began to calm him. Tonight he would not dream.

Katyesha was long in coming.

"War is mathematics," Ab Drem said. "The best discipline." He continued aloud to someone invisible, "Woman, our daughter is to marry." His voice was almost tender. "You broke me, but she will heal me."

At that instant the latch rattled softly and Katyesha stepped across the threshold. She bore the yoke, and the muted browns and grays of her clothing were as drab as a mallard hen; yet her face was flushed and rosy and Ab Drem saw her as more beautiful than ever his wife had been, finer than the chancellor at War. He rose without a word and lifted the buckets from the chains. Why, they were heavy! He set them down with a splash, saying, "That is too much for you to carry!"

She stepped backward and said uncertainly, "I carry it every day." As though he were not there, she reached around him, retrieved the buckets and hefted them easily to the hearth. Without looking up, she said, "I'm sorry I'm late, sir. The dark came soon."

"The longest night." How should he tell her? He could not talk to women; he had never been able to talk to her mother. He had such joy to give her

135

and no way to give it. Moving back to the game board, he took up the white chancellor. At last he said, "This long night you will remember."

She looked up at him, alarmed.

He was annoyed. What did women think? Did they have minds? What should she fear? He rapped with his fingers on the board, so that the gamesmen jumped.

She had been taught never to talk back, but tonight she faced him with her hands tangled in the gray folds of her skirt. "Why?" she said.

He was taken aback; but he recovered himself and in a rush gave to her all that he had held for her since her infancy, all that she brought to him. "Daughter, you're to be married!"

"Married?" Color like fire rushed over her, even her ears, her freckled hands.

"You are to be married!"

"Who?"

Naturally she would want to know. And what he could tell her! Not to a grocer, a stonemason, a clerk. "To Ab Harlan's son!"

"Who?"

Damn them! When you asked reason of them they were emotional, or they were thinking of something else. With annoyance he repeated, "To Ab Harlan's son. To . . . ah, the name . . . Queelic. To Queelic!"

Like an echo the wind whined in the chimney and puffed ashes over the hearth. He waited for her gratitude, her shy joy.

But she raised herself back as a snake does. She snatched the kerchief from her head as though it galled her, and her short hair stood up scarlet in the light from the fire.

"Him?" she cried. "I'll never!"

"What?" he said foolishly, holding the chancellor in his hand.

"I'll never marry him. Not him!"

"Stop it!" cried Ab Drem. The mood was spoiled. Though his gift to her might be retrieved and polished again, she had tarnished it. He was furious.

"No!" she said, and before his unbelieving eyes she hurled the kerchief into the fire. She tugged at the ties to her cloak and threw it off also, as though it shackled her. "I'll never marry. I won't! I'll have my man."

"What are you saying!"

"I won't live here. I won't marry him. I'll have my man instead!"

"Hussy! Shameless!" cried Ab Drem in pain; and suddenly, "You are like your mother!"

"I hope I am!"

It was not true, what was happening. To pacify her, to mend the thing, he said, "You'll sleep in silk, my daughter."

"I'd rather sleep in the cow blanket with him!"

Carefully he set down the chancellor. "What? Who?"

She stopped, as though she had frightened herself. Then she hurled it out recklessly, free. "Nall!"

"Nall? Nall?"

She flinched to hear that name from his mouth, but her own bravado carried her forward. "You know him! You cast him out!"

"I! Nall!"

"Take that thing Downshore, you said."

"What? Thing? *That?*"

"Stop it!" She raised both her hands together, as a bear does.

"That was a dirty animal!"

"He is not! He is not!"

Blind with rage and disappointment, he advanced upon her. She backed away from him until she stood nearly in the fire.

"It does not end," he said softly, beside himself. "One begins it blindly and it never ends."

"My mother was not bad," the girl cried. "She was not bad!"

He had her trapped; but to his disbelief she stepped forward toward him, her face upturned beneath his own. "Nall is not bad either," she hissed. "I love him. He is my man!"

"Slut!" The word was wrenched from him. "Have you slept with that beast?"

Caught off guard, she said candidly, "I . . . I *slept* with him."

He had not meant to hit her. But out of the ruins of his redemption his hand rose and struck her across the mouth.

She fell back against the mantel with her hands to her face.

She would wed Ab Harlan's son if he had to beat her into it, if he had to lock her in her box bed until her wedding day. He stepped forward, raising his arm.

But she straightened, catching both his wrists. "No," she said.

He twisted his arms to break her grip but to his horror he could not. She was his child, his baby; yet he could not move his hands.

They stood deadlocked in the groan of the wind, she looking at him over her bloodied mouth.

"Let me go," he said at last. "Let me go."

She did not loose him, but an uncertainty came over her face, as though she realized what it was she did. In that instant he lunged backward, jerking his wrists free.

He staggered straight into the gaming table, tipping the board with its ranked armies onto the flagstone floor. The glassy crash of porcelain broke brightly over the wind's whine; bits of legs and helmets, faces and swords splashed across the stones. The white chancellor's body was splinters and dust. Only his head, colorless and stern, lay whole in the shambles.

"Ai," said Ab Drem. "Ai."

It was a child's voice, seeing all ruined. He stood.

There was a ghost of movement at the periphery of his stare, the crackling scuff of a boot treading a shattered slave, the yelp of a hinge. Ab Drem stared at the chancellor's face. He heard the door latch click, then silence, except for the wind and the small noises of the fire.

It was Long Night, the longest night, when all the animals dance.

18

Her blood tasted of salt. She could not feel her mouth, which her father had struck, nor her hands, which had gripped his wrists so he could not move them. She held the wedding clothes that she had snatched from the chest but she could not feel them either, and had to look down to find the embroidered bear, black in the starlight and all but invisible in the darkness of the byre.

Nor could she feel her feet, and stumbled in the straw. She must say good-bye to Moss; but to speak would make it real, so she was silent.

Moss turned her heavy head. The old gray tom

sat surly on the cow's shoulder; as Kat took him up he spat. With Small Gray clamped under one elbow Kat left Upslope, kicking the byre door shut.

Small Gray did not like the wind and fumed, lashing his tail. At the first turn of the cattle path he writhed so that she almost dropped the wedding clothes; as she stopped to hitch the bundle higher he clawed free, bounding back up the footpath in the dark.

"Small Gray!" she cried. "Small Gray!" But he was gone. She shouted after him, "They won't love you there!" and turned her face downward again, running, because for an instant she had felt her fingers and her mouth. She had remembered the feel of her father's wrists, his dry old skin loose on the bone.

"I'm not that strong!" she sobbed aloud.

The houses on the cattle path were deserted. No life but watchdogs guarded the darkened hearths, but when she raised her eyes from her flying feet she saw a swarm of lights on the beach, torch and fire, with Downshore dark against the hills beyond it. The wind set softly from the north and she heard, faintly, the Year Drum: *boom, boom,* like something walking.

She would not listen. There was nobody in her skin to dance. She was empty, without mouth or feet or hands, nothing but a name that had meant obedient, prudent, Ab Drem's daughter—and she had overthrown her name.

In the night without boundaries she stumbled among the middens and the pigsties toward the other name she knew.

"Katyesha n'Ab Nall," she sobbed under her breath.

The moon was not yet above the cliffs. She came to the beach well south of the great gathering and turned away from it. Mailin's house was black and cold, and that lightless light was on the sea.

At the foot of the steps she halted in a smoke of fear. All was so still, except for her breath raking in her chest; though she might have clattered up the wide boards she hunched, gripping the wedding clothes, and crept up one step at a time as though not to try the silence.

As she stepped onto the balcony Nall's voice said, "Kat!" so near to her body that she cried out and leapt away.

He sat on the edge of the verandah, a dark shape under the railing. "Kat," he said again.

When she could speak she gasped, "You are supposed to be at the hearth," and did not know her own voice.

"All hearths are dark tonight."

She could just make out the black shape of his body.

His eyes glittered. He said, "You came to dance?"

"No."

She needed him to call her: "Come to me!" But he did not; after a moment she could not wait for it and said it for him in her heart. But her feet would not move. She felt his eyes on her, and involuntarily she put one hand up to cover her mouth.

He had seen it. He said sharply: "Who struck you?"

"My father." She had a flashing image of Nall standing before Ab Drem, short and strong, his brown fist quick, Ab Drem reeling.

But Nall said only, "Here is water to wash it."

Because he would not command her, she could not be obedient; she must take the next best thing and pretend that he had. Though her body cringed from him she came close, and knelt down.

He had a stone jar of cold tea. In the dark he was shadowy as a demon. With his bare hand he washed her mouth, and his face was a stranger's.

He is kind, she told herself. My man. But she did not know him.

His voice was steadfast, clear. "Why did he strike you?"

She opened her mouth to say, For you! but the words stuck. Instead she cried, "I can't go back to Upslope!"

For an instant she saw how it would be from now on: getting Nall's porridge, sweeping his hearth, mending his coat. But he had no coat.

"Where will you go?"

"I could stay with you," she said.

His expression did not change. It was interested, quiet. As he said nothing, panic rose in her, and haste and shame, and she stammered, "I could keep your hearth. I can cook, I can sew."

He said nothing.

Her heart dwindled and died, until in a whisper

she finished, "You would not have to marry me. You could be . . . I would be just your girl."

She felt as mice must feel before the cat takes them, perhaps happy to be food for cats; she saw his shoulders shift as he leaned forward.

"Swim," he said.

She gawked. "What?"

"Swim," he repeated in his clear voice. "If you are swimming you must swim. You must not grab at another swimmer, or both will drown."

She looked at him as though it were not the Plain tongue he spoke.

He said, "Are you my slave?"

She snatched herself backward from him. "I am not your slave!"

"Are you my daughter?" The voice was inexorable, interested, sad. "May I strike you when you do not do my will?"

"Stop it!" she cried.

"Swim for yourself."

"I can't swim!"

"Swim!"

She scrambled to her feet. From the dark at the top of the stairs she cried out, "I hate you! I hate all of you!" and snatching up the stone jar of tea she flung it at him.

He caught it neatly, one-handed, and as she rattled down the stairs he rose. Looking back once over her shoulder she saw him against the paler sky, solid and small.

"Katyesha!"

"That's not my name!"

"I will wait for you," he called after her in his clear voice. "I will meet you on the other side of the water."

She might have run toward the dance, but everyone there had homes and names. She ran toward the dark, southward down the empty beach. Almost flying, like a bird that is chivvied from branch to branch, she ran through the cobbles and soft sand to Horn Loft and past it, out of the protection of the bay. She ran to the nameless beach where it had begun, huddling her mother's wedding clothes against her breasts.

The beach was dark, empty of all life. There was no seal, no man; the black rocks collared with shining foam were bare. At the far end of the strand rose the Upslope path—but she could not take that path.

She ran to the middle of the sandy curve and there halted, as though her feet knew there was no way out and stopped for her. That ghostly light was on the sea; the land was dead and empty, and the sea alive.

She faced it cloakless, sobbing. Her mouth hurt like her heart. She could feel her fingers and feet now but they were cold, cold.

The sea had washed away Nall's draggled turtle trail as though it had never been. With the whole ferocity of despair she wished herself back three days to safety, to the barren familiar hearth; but that hearth was lost to her. The gray tide beat at the gray sand in fists and splinters, in long waves.

She turned to walk straight out into the water, to drown. Partly because there was no house for her, no name, and partly to prove that among all her wrongness she was right in one thing: She could not swim. But she was so cold already that this vaster coldness would absorb her as it would a raindrop; she cringed from it. The tree trunk that she had climbed two days before lay unchanged above the wrack; she stumbled into its lee and in the hollow of its roots she curled into a ball, like an animal with nothing to protect itself but its skin.

She thought: I don't even know how to die.

She held her breath.

The wind piped in the naked roots; the water pushed empty shells to and fro on the sand.

She thought suddenly of the twin babies, dead in the cold, who had decided to be seals. Aloud she cried, *"What am I supposed to be?"*

For something had changed, a very little: From having been as wholly cold as a stone, a little warmth had begun in the middle of the clenched fist of herself. It spread very slowly through her thighs and chest. It was like the banked fire that Mailin had left to weather the longest night.

She reached back to tuck in her inadequate shirt. She sobbed, *"Mailin* has her own house!"

On this unearthly beach her voice sounded impiously cross and plain. Yet nothing vengeful came coiling out of the water. She curled around her own small warmth as though it were a hearth, a child not born that she would name when she saw its face. Raising her head, she watched the sea.

On the white sand the waves took shape, lost shape, patiently changing.

She rose stiffly.

Walking down to the waves, she thrust her hand into the racing foam and brought it wet to her mouth.

It was salty, like blood. It stung her lip.

She untied her boots, carried them above the tideline, and left them with her wool stockings neatly folded on the wedding clothes; on her bare white feet she approached the water.

So sharp the cold! The waves startled her ankles with wet strokes, the surge incessantly moving, tugging like a hand. But she was warm.

"I don't need him," she said aloud. "I'll find out by myself."

Her clothes were tight and heavy. She stripped off her shirt and threw it broadly backward, out of reach of the water, and then her skirt, her shift, her drawers. Firm-footed as a fishing bear she waded westward, testing each step before she took it, cold to her white knees.

Thigh-deep she halted. It was so big, the unknown world welling from the horizon. She thought, From this he came! From this!

She knelt down with a shudder in the rocking water.

She was stroked, held everywhere: more than by her mother, more than by his absent hand. A wave doused her; she sneezed and spat bitterness. Her hair was as dark as his had been, plastered to her head.

The waves lifted her firmly from her knees and set her back. At each surge she waved her feet a little, her hands a little, not quite swimming but practicing to swim the way a baby seal, unborn in its mother's belly, must practice: readying to make that plunge at last into the rolling dark, to speed along dim water paths toward far islands. . . .

She stood up. "I can't yet," she said. "But I could learn."

The ocean surged between her thighs, that long wave stronger and older than he was. Turning, she carried her warmth out of the lessening swell, licking the salt from her wrist.

Shaking with life and cold, she took up the shirt that was too small and dried herself. She made a carrying bundle of it for her skirt and shift, and put on her mother's wedding clothes—so that if that man whose life she had saved should look seaward from Mailin's house, he would see striding past him not the girl who had needed him but a Hill woman, walking like a queen.

19

IT SOUNDED LIKE THE SEA but it was flesh, the human tide that rolled upon the Downshore beach. Its foam was the hiss of voices in the dark, and the jostle of bodies was the slap of waves; over all boomed the Year Drum like an invariable surf.

The drum had been rolled out as the sun was westering, and among much argument about which way the sparks would blow it was dropped on its empty side with a boom. The first two drummers, woman and man, had taken their seats on either side; each took up two drumsticks. They stretched, settled their shoulders, planted their feet and rubbed their noses with the backs of their hands. As the last glint of sun winked out on the western sea they began the beat that would continue all night long: left, right, left, right, the great padded drumsticks striking the hide so perfectly, two and two, that the drum might have been a huge heart beating without pause. As each drummer tired another of the same sex would come to take the empty chair, so that throughout the night the unerring beat would thin to one set of drumsticks, then double again to two, like a heart that moves farther away and then returns. This was the drum Kat had heard on the down-bound cattle path, that she heard now as she strode toward the unlit Year Fire. It passed each crisis with its perfect beat unbroken, like the heart of the world that beats through every age and season undisturbed by year's end or year's return. It would not cease until the morning sun.

In and out of the flicker and snap of torches and the side-fires' blustering sough, Kat walked toward the drum bare-headed, in wedding clothes.

She would look for the Hill women, and ask about her mother.

There were raucous drunks along the fringes of the crowd but she had slipped past them, following that steady thunder out of the ocean dark into the multitudinous glare of carnival. Afraid to stop, she strode dazzled past torch and brazier, past the looming roof of the Year Fire's stack, until she could see the rise and fall of the double drumsticks. All the music of the carnival, flute and bones and fiddle and knuckle drum, entwined that beat; keeping it, fighting it, embellishing it, losing it and finding it again.

Kat braced herself in the wash of sound. Rocked and bullied, she guarded her small warmth as the tide of noise rose higher and broke over her head. The drumsticks rose and plunged like oars, like swimmers' arms; she began to panic and to think: Mailin! Dai! She searched for them futilely in the sea of faces, terrified that she would drown.

But she could almost swim. In the crackling shadow of a windy canopy she found her feet again and straightened her back, drawing smoother breath.

She said doggedly, "I must look for red hair." With that as her talisman she turned from the drum back into the confusion of the crowd, hunting resolutely among unknown jovial faces until she saw, in a tangle of children sharing a stolen pie under a table, a red-haired boy.

She bent down to him; she spoke the only words she knew of the Hill tongue. *"Katim na, O!"*

He scrambled out, startled, chattering in a foreign torrent.

"Wait!" she cried in the Plain tongue. "I can't speak that!"

"Why not?" he piped, shifting to common speech. "You are a bear!"

"A bear? . . ."

"You are *dressed* like a bear." He pointed to her skirt, her embroidered blouse.

"Where are the Hill women?" said Kat.

Without hesitation he took her hand, and together they plowed into the crowd. He tugged her boldly past hawkers and fiddlers, past children playing Scissors Paper Stone, past the brewers' rig where the great barrels dripped from their spigots into the sand. Children swarmed on crudely painted roundabouts; in the bakers' booth, men in sacking aprons prodded fritters in the steamy grease, and the customers licked their fingers. She knew no one. She walked in utter trust, led by that small hand and flashes of red hair.

And then it was as though they came into the shelter of a rock. He halted, leaning against her.

"Here's my mother," he said. "Ma!"

The rock was a group of women in dark skirts, standing as unconcerned in the chaos as Horn Loft with its feet in foam. At the boy's shout they turned, laughing. He tugged Kat stumbling into the torchlight; in final, futile panic she put up her free hand as though with it she could hide her bright hair.

The voices were amazed, foreign, multitudinous. A woman stepped forward. She had no head covering but her coiled red braid. Like the other women she wore an embroidered skirt and blouse, less fine than Kat's; Kat could not see the patterns clearly but she knew them: bears, marmots, a tomtit.

"*Ouma*," Kat heard among the surf of words. "*Katim na!*"

With dignity the boy announced in the Plain tongue, "She cannot talk like a bear. She said so."

"What bear comes among us, dressed for a wedding?"

Kat looked at her hands. They were still human, even the one the child had held.

The woman's hair was like a crown. Lifting a torch from another hand she raised it over Kat's head, and its light drenched both of them.

"You are dressed as a Bear of the Circle," she said at last. Her voice was clear and concerned, like her face. "Who are you?"

There was no name to give but the old one. Instead Kat said, "The clothes were my mother's."

"Who is she?"

"I don't know."

A murmur moved among the crowd of women. Delighted with this drama, the boy squirmed to look up at Kat, and together they made a still place in the middle of the roaring carnival.

Kat said, "She came from the hills."

There were quiet glances. A voice spoke from beyond the torchlight: "Tell us her name!"

"They never told me."

"Is she dead?"

"Yes."

A woman who was suckling her child shifted it from one breast to the other, and it wailed. Slipping his hand from Kat's, the boy leaned on his mother; she smoothed his hair. "Then tell us of her what you have," she said.

These were Kat's last treasures, and she spent them all together. "She had red hair. She used to rock us. She sang that song, the bear one: There was me, *katim na*, and my brother was *katim yao*. She was beautiful, they said. She . . . she married. Upslope."

It was such a meager hoard! When she had

squandered it she stopped, appalled that she had so bankrupted herself to strangers. And she could tell them nothing of what was really important: the memory of a heavy and warm arm.

A whisper began among the women, a word repeated. Giving the torch to another, the boy's mother reached out and set one hand under Kat's chin. Her eyes looked here and there at Kat's face, her skirt, the bright yoke of her blouse.

"Your father," she asked, "he was Upslope?"

Now that the moment had come, Kat was in horror of it; but she answered, "Yes."

"Tell us of your father," the woman said sharply. "Was he slender, golden? Was he fierce and very shy, reckless with too much wine? As he rode, did he sing? Tell!"

Reprieve and disappointment swept over Kat like a breaker, black. "Oh, no!" she cried. "My father is old. He is thin and cruel and ugly. He has bad dreams."

"His name was Drem."

"Ab Drem." She brought it out, unbelieving. "Ab . . . Drem." And violently, "It's not him. He wasn't like that, never!"

"She was carrying his child; she went with him. She quarreled with our father. These are her clothes, Lisei's—I helped her to embroider them. You are my sister's child!"

"Lisei! Lisei!" That was the word the women spoke. "Lisei!" The red-haired woman looked at Kat with her face filling with light, like morning.

154

Kat stepped back. "No!" she said savagely—to all of it, to the firm hand on her arm, to the sudden possession of a history; but most of all to the image of her father young and eager, her father like . . . Nall. "No!"

The woman did not seem to hear her, asking a question as though she had carried it brimming in her heart for years, and now must pour it. "Why did she not come back? We heard nothing, even from the messenger. Was it so much, that quarrel? We loved her. To show us the baby—why not?"

"It died. That baby died."

"All the more. Oh, my Lisei!"

"It was a demon. It had a bear's face."

The murmur was not horror, but pity. "My poor Lisei!" Another voice said, "Poor Drem."

The woman took Kat's hands into her own. "That was not a demon. That was just a bear's-face child." As though to comfort Kat were to comfort the dead Lisei, she said earnestly, "Were you so young and hurt among the ignorant? Such children come to bless us. They remind us that we are kin to the beasts, who are innocent; then they go back to the Mother. To live in two worlds would be hard for them."

"They bring us luck," someone offered from the dark. "Or storms."

The circle of faces shone interested and compassionate and kind. Very gently, Kat's new aunt touched her cheek. "Was it your father who split your lip?"

Kat nodded.

"I will wager you did not let him hit you more than once."

"No," said Kat slowly. "Only once."

Her aunt's hands were as strong as her own. They might have come from the same maker, they were so alike in breadth and knuckle and thumb.

"I am Bian, your mother's sister. I do not know your name, but with my whole heart I welcome you, *katim na.*"

"That's my name. You said it."

"Katim na?"

"Yes. But I call myself Kat."

20

THE FIRST HORN of the moon rose above the cliffs.

The Hill women had painted each other's faces with bear's fat, charcoal, and white clay, in the patterns of the bear. Kat's face was black and silver. She stared dazed at the blade of moonlight, her hands to her bare head.

"My hair is so short. . . ."

"It is growing," said Bian. She was painting claw stripes on her son's knuckles. "Will you come back with us? Come to the hills where your mother was

157

born, and see *ouma* and *katim na* in the meadow. If you stay here your father will look for you."

"I . . . maybe."

"What is it? Do you have a man? But we leave our men in the hills when we come here to the sea. Leave him for a little, just a little, and come to the hills with us."

"I don't have a man."

Around them the crowd was almost still. The drum spoke.

Like a boat that slips from harbor the moon slid from the rocks and sailed westward, free.

An eager murmur passed, like the ripple from a flung stone. The crowd surged forward, then poured back. Bian snatched Kat's hand, and they stumbled backward with the rest as the first of the dancers swung out from town.

In the juddering torchlight they did not look like men and women marked with ash and clay. Their gray skins glinted. They were gray seals swimming, diving, dodging, streaming from the ancient alleys of Downshore toward the dark house of the year. From the crowd around them rose other dancers— fox and orca, bear and eagle, badger and otter and gull. Later they would sing their own songs, but in this first moment they joined in the oldest music, the song for crossing. The Rigi's song.

> *I am a man upon the land,*
> *I am a beast upon the deep,*
> *I am the fin that hides the hand,*
> *I am the dream that riddles sleep.*

I am the wind that breaks the door,
I am the pulse that fans the pain,
I am the wave that grinds the shore,
I am the rock that turns the rain. . . .

Kat reeled in the chanting press; Bian's hand steadied her. The song poured from a thousand mouths.

"I have to dance that!" she sobbed. "I have to dance for . . . I have to dance the Seal!"

"Lali!" A gray shape rose; Kat darted forward, and in Mailin's hard embrace the great sealskin wrapped them both.

"I thought to find you with your own," said Mailin.

"Teach me the Seal. Mailin, teach me the Seal!"

"But she is a *bear!*" cried Bian's young son, outraged. "She is all painted to be a bear!"

Bian laughed, Mailin laughed; their eyes were the same.

Beyond Mailin's shoulder Kat saw Pao with his stiff-kneed shuffle, Suni with her man at her elbow, Rosie smiling on her father's hip. The blaze of the badger was on all their foreheads.

"She is who she is," said Bian. "Seal, bear . . . go, sister's daughter. Dance for your friend, I see him in your eyes. And I shall dance for my Lisei, for her bear's-face child."

Kat said, "I don't know who I dance for."

"Lali!" Mailin's eyes shone bright, imperturbable in her painted face. "To find out for whom you dance: Dance!"

159

No one in particular kindled it. It was time. Maybe it was a child, prompted by her cousin, who ran squealing from the side-fires with the first burning branch and thrust it into the very edge of the towering house of the year.

Sparks jumped. Then many torches came; there was such haste to cast the side-fires into the Year Fire that for a moment there was a wave of color from the periphery into the dark center, and then the center bloomed. The hoarded wood was so dry that it went up like tinder, the flames standing in the night sky like a pillar in a dream. They blazed on the upturned faces that roared back with open mouths.

Then the real dancing began.

There was music at every hand: fiddle and bagpipe and horn, not a cacophony but an immense unceasing interresponding reverberation like the sea. Everywhere was motion, jig and swing. Children bobbed and twirled, their hands raised like forepaws or spread like wings. Old ladies danced the Long Night for the last time, on two canes. The striped awnings fluttered netherworld colors in the dark and fire; the flames flattened and rumpled in the wind, kicking sparks into the crowd. Sometimes in circles, sometimes in lines, the dancers swung closer to the fire as the flames died in one place, or drew back as someone came bearing one last old mattress or broken bough to make the blaze rise up again. There were many small decisions to be rid of things: a book, a bowl, a bottle flung into the fire.

The Lake tribes danced the Mouse, the Wild

Dog, and the Swan. The River men danced the Muskrat, smoothing their mustaches. Other tribes danced the Hawk, the Otter, the Deer, the Wolf, the Dove; one cross old man in a white-striped tailcoat danced the Skunk. Those who had no clan or calling danced gravely or wildly, according to their hearts.

The men from Upslope came. They only watched. Booted and correct, they bunched at the crowd's edge and drank from flasks of their own brandy, their faces tense and avid, speaking among themselves of this woman or that. This year one came alone, a long, lean man who strode among the painted faces as though he searched; but he found nothing, and after a while he went away. The children whispered among themselves that he was Death, because of his face.

"Dai! Dai!"

He danced clumsily and solemnly, as a cow might dance. He was dancing with a Downshore girl in a blue bodice; it was a moment before he knew Kat in those clothes, in that place. He loosed the girl and she spun away laughing.

"Sister!"

Flames lit them: flaring, sinking, always changing. Kat held a parcel under one arm. She said, "I've left Cliff Tooth House."

He seemed unsurprised, solemnly lumbering. She added, "I've met the Hill women. I've found our aunt. I've changed my big name, Dai: I'm *Katim na.*"

"Like *katim yao*," he said, approving. "Ah!"

The heat of the fire was like a wall. She held up the damp bundle of her clothes. "I'm throwing them in."

"Waste . . ."

"I know." She hurled them into the whitest place; it was too bright to look.

"Ah!" When Dai tried to dance without moving forward he bobbed, and other dancers banged him on the back. He dragged his old gray jersey over his head, crying, "Katyesha made this! Katyesha Marashya n'Ab Drem!"

He flung it high; like a moth it flew toward the light and vanished.

"Or whoever you are," he said. "Sister's what I call you."

He took a great firm hold on her fist, and they danced.

The drum boomed; the moon rolled on; Kat danced.

She danced for Nall, loyally, with Mailin: dancing the Seal, the dark torrents of the current, the breakers, the dim roads of the sea. But she left that dance, and in the rooted rocky vaults of the mountains she danced the Bear, lumbering shank and shoulder with Bian at her elbow.

And then she left that dance. She danced alone.

Who am I? Who was I before my parents, before my skin, my hair, my name?

She danced until in the dancing there was no future and no past. She became herself, nameless beyond name, plain as a blade of grass, a star.

She began to cry, not the outbursts of before but just tears, very ordinary, very clean; they streaked the grease and ashes on her face. She danced her own dance. These were her legs that stamped, her hands that clapped, her voice that sang—sometimes the Rigi's song, sometimes the bear's growl, sometimes a new music, hers, that came to her. It was the tiny central seed of a song, one line only, sturdy and firm:

I have two feet, hey!
I have two feet, hey!

She stamped and sang, under the tower of the fire.

21

IT WAS A CHILLY, brilliant day.

The sun shone. At the tide's edge, gravel growled in the undertow with hush and wash, hiss and sigh; sandpipers cried along the water. Scattered here and there on the bright sand, sleepers snored insignificantly in the grand morning; half-waked and carried, children wailed in voices tinier than the birds'.

The drum stood mute. Its last drummers slept beside it in the light, hats over their faces. From the scar of the Year Fire a coil of smoke rose lazily into the blue air; the ashes clicked as they cooled. Along the water's edge, Kat splashed toward Mailin's house, her bare feet making a racket in the sea.

He was where she had thought he would be.

In her mind's eye last night she had seen him: restless and, hearing the dim drum, taking the cow blanket and the hoe and setting off toward the sea. Now he sat on the empty sand above the tide line, his chin on his raised knee, watching the winter ocean. As crutch he had taken the shovel, not the hoe.

Because the beach was curved he had seen Kat splashing every step along the lip of the water from the Year Fire's smoking scar, yet he had not moved. Perhaps he did not know her? Her face was very dirty, and she wore the wedding clothes. Yet he must know her. She hunkered down at a safe distance, waiting for him to call her by her name.

He did not. Only after a moment he raised his head from his knee, and smiled.

She wondered whether this was a battle, a war of waiting. Then she decided that she was not fighting. With dignity she said, "Nall."

His smile deepened, as though it sank back into his bones. "Kat!"

That was her name; though he might know it, he would never know all of her. And she would never know all of him, just as she would never know all of the sea. Uncertainly she nodded and said, "But it means something different than it did."

His smile became a grin, with its broken tooth. She was reminded of the morning sun swelling over the cliffs, when the drum stopped. "Good dance?" he said.

"Good dance."

The wind wreathed back and forth between them. "I danced the Seal," she said. "I danced the Bear. Nall—I danced."

He said softly, "We are so many, in one skin."

The gulls' crying was lonely, hung in the endless air. Hesitantly he held out half the blanket, as a bird holds out its wing.

"I don't need to be your girl." She was stiff with shame, but did not drop her eyes.

"No. That we may both be warm."

Her heart despaired in her. But she came and sat next to him, not touching him, under the old cow blanket.

It did not smell like Moss anymore but like him, like a young cat come from hunting; she breathed the male smell of him at every breath.

He looked at her anxiously. She was not used to that look on him. Yesterday he would have touched her, but now he kept his good hand on his knee.

He said, "I am not keeping you."

"I know." She tucked up her cold feet and wrapped herself in her half of the blanket. After a moment she said crossly, "Ch-h-h!" and settled her shoulder against his.

He kept his hand on his knee. She looked at the rope marks on his wrist. "Aren't you angry? That they did that."

"I did that to myself, getting free."

166

"If they hadn't tied you, you wouldn't have had to break away!"

"If they had not tied me," he said simply, "I would not have gone with them."

She laughed; he gave her his hand, smiling. "They took me to the Place of Bones. That was good; from the Home Stone it would have been too far to swim. For them the Place of Bones is the end of the world."

"It's the end of *this* world. After that there's nothing but things that drown you, and the Rigi."

"It is the beginning of this world."

She thought of Lisei, Bian, the unknown hills. "I don't think the world has ends."

"Good!" he said with satisfaction.

Aching, she drew breath to speak. But he was looking out to sea with a sharpened glance; she turned and saw three dark small heads, like swimmers' heads, lost and found among the waters.

She gripped his hand.

"Only seals," he said. He gazed beyond the swimming specks, westward, to where the sea was empty.

"Winter," he said. "The gray straight rain. We sleep, we dream. Mothers with the smallest children in the middle; the rest of us, the strong ones, on the outside to keep them warm. Even so, it is cold. We die, many of us. From dreaming we dive into death." He turned his head sideways, his cheek on his knee, so that he could not look except at her. His face was remote and full of grief. "Yet I am here alive, and it is warm."

"You chose to swim!"

His smile came back. "Your name now means what thing?"

"*Katim na*, for Cub, the bear's child."

He laughed, and with his old easiness he put his hand up to her face. "I said so! That red bear!"

"Oh, don't! Don't!" She pulled her face away from him and put it down on her knees; then raised it. "I'm going away. I have to, I said I would. Nall . . ."

He said nothing, his hand poised; she took it, saying, "I'll go tomorrow with my aunt, to the hills where my mother came from."

"You are going away?"

She clasped his fist hard against her chest. "I don't know anything," she cried. "I have to learn. You know that—I can't be just part of somebody else!"

And that would be the end of it: The man, like the wave, would turn, drawing back from her down the beaches of the world, leaving her sturdy and desolate.

But he looked at her as he had in the dark of the travelers' rest, saying slowly, "You are more wonderful than the sun."

She could not answer. His hand lay between hers, momentarily part of her.

"You know many things already," he said. "But . . . in the hills will you see bears?"

"She says so. My aunt."

"When you have seen, learned, then . . . you will come back to this shore? To me?"

She felt him breathe. The chill of winter snouted in wherever the blanket was not tucked.

168

"I don't know. Oh, don't ask me! I want to! But it all keeps changing, changing all the time."

"You are swimming!" he cried in delight. "You can swim!"

He took his hand away from her, laughing, and reaching around her lightly he kissed her mouth.

"Ow!" she said, because of her cut lip.

She looked at him as though from deep waters— some of them the tidal abandon of joy, some of them a safe familiar dread. "Do I have to swim to the other side of the water?" she said. "It will be strange there."

"I will sing the Rigi's song for you. The new part, mine. I will call you from that shore."

"Sing it, then! So that I'll know it. Sing it now!"

He looked away from her, shyly, or as though he asked permission from someone unseen; turning back he raised his head, and sang.

> I am the ash that snuffs the fire,
> I am the knot that halts the loom,
> I am the tangle of desire,
> I am the love that clouds the womb.
>
> I am the sigh that stills the scream,
> I am the word that frees the dumb,
> I am the light that ends the dream.
> I am the child. I come, I come.

His harsh and certain voice poured around her like water, and withdrew. She crouched, drenched, in the silence of its ebb.

"All right," she said doggedly. "But I won't come unless I feel like it."

"Good!"

It was warmer to sit between his knees where he could hold her, his rough jaw against her ear; she held his hand to her face.

Behind them under Mailin's porch the black cow mooed, and with it another cow.

"Nall! That's Moss!"

"All this morning they shout, shout. Too much. Maybe I shall have to go to the hills with you."

The tide was going out. They sat together the way seals sit, or bears, that dream all winter.